All Set About
with Fever Trees

All Set About with Fever Trees

and Other Stories

Pam Durban

DAVID R. GODINE

Publisher · Boston

First published in 1985 by
David R. Godine, Publisher, Inc.
306 Dartmouth Street
Boston, Massachusetts 02116

LIBRARY OF CONGRESS CATALOGING IN PUBLICATION DATA

Durban, Pam.
    All set about with fever trees.

    I. Title.
PS3554.U668A4   1985   813'.54   84-48749
ISBN 0-87923-569-1

Ohio Arts Council **Individual Artist**
Fellowship Recipient/FY 1984

First edition

Printed in the United States of America

For my mother and father

THE STORIES in this book, now much revised, first appeared in the following periodicals. The author is grateful to these publications for permission to reprint. "Made to Last" (under the title "Let Me Not to the Marriage"), *Tri-Quarterly*, #51, Spring 1981. "World of Women," *Epoch*, Fall 1980. "Notes Toward an Understanding of My Father's Novel," *Ohio Review* #25, reprinted in the Tenth Anniversary Issue, Fall 1983. "In Darkness," *Crazyhorse*, Fall 1982. "This Heat," *The Georgia Review*, Summer 1982. "All Set About with Fever Trees," *The Georgia Review*, Summer 1984.

The author is also grateful for the help she received from the following groups and institutions during the writing of this book: the Mary Roberts Rinehart Foundation; the Ohio Arts Council for a 1983–84 Individual Artists Grant; the University of Iowa Writers' Workshop for a James Michener Fellowship from the Copernicus Society of America; Ohio University for its generosity in granting leaves of absence; the Isaac W. Bernheim Foundation Forest and its manager, Mac McClure.

Contents

This Heat

IN AUGUST, Beau Clinton died. He was playing basketball in the high-school gym and when his bad heart set him free he staggered and fell, he blew one bloody bubble that lingered, shimmering, until it burst, sprinkling blood like rust spots, all over his pale face. The school phoned Ruby Clinton but they wouldn't say what the trouble was, just that Beau was sick, in trouble, something — it was all the same trouble — and could Ruby or Mr. Clinton come right down. "Isn't any Mr. Clinton," Ruby snapped, but the woman had already hung up the phone. So she figured she'd best go down to see what he'd done this time, her son who looked so much like his sorry father, Charles Clinton, it was all she could do sometimes to keep from tearing into him.

Ruby walked down the hall working herself up for the next showdown with Beau or the principal or whoever crossed her. No one made her angrier than Beau. She could get so angry that bright points of light danced in front of her eyes. Of course it didn't matter, not at all; she might as well rave at the kudzu, tell it to stop climbing on everything and choking it, hauling it down under those deadly green vines. A woman with a worried face directed Ruby to the clinic room and Ruby quickened her step. But when she

3

got there, a man blocked the doorway. "You can't go in there," he said. Ruby didn't answer and she didn't stop. She was used to plowing past men such as he, and she knew her strength in these matters. There were things in this life that wouldn't give, that was a fact, but you put your shoulder against them and you shoved anyway.

"The hell you say," Ruby said. "If he's having one of his spells I know what to do."

"He's not having one of his spells," the man said. "I'm afraid he's dead."

She squinted and watched while the man collapsed into a tiny man and then grew life-size again. She had a steady mannish face, and when something stunned her that face turned smooth and still, as if everything had been hoarded and boarded up back of her eyes somewhere. Younger, she'd had a bold way of memorizing people, but that look had narrowed until she looked as if she were squinting to find something off in the distance. She'd been what they call *hot-blooded*, a fighter, all her people were fierce and strong, good people to have on your side. There was once something of the gypsy about her – a lancing eye and tongue and the gypsy darkness shot through with a ruby light. But that seemed like a long time ago. Now, at the time of Beau's death, Ruby was thirty-two, but she looked worn and strong. Her face had settled into a thick heavy grain like wood left lying outside since the day it was first split from the tree.

She'd gone there ready to scream at Beau, to smack him good for whatever he'd done, to drag him away from a fight one more time – he'd sat right there and heard what the judge had said – or from playing ball – he'd heard the

4

doctor say that he was not to move faster than a walk if he wanted to live through the summer. She'd gone there ready to smack him, breathing harshly through her nose. She still had faith in the habit of hitting him — it roused him for a second or two, raised him out of the daze where he lived most of the time — a numb sort of habit that began as pressure behind her eyes and ended with the blunt impact and the sound of the flat of her hand landing hard against his skull.

The words she would have said and the sound of the blow she'd gone ready to deliver echoed and died in her head. Words rushed up and died in her throat — panicked words, words to soothe, to tame, to call him back — they rushed on her, but she forgot them halfway to her mouth and he lay so still. And that's how she learned that Beau Clinton, her only son and the son of Charles Clinton, was dead.

From then on it was just one amazement after another. She was amazed to find the day just as hot and close as it had been when she'd gone inside the school building. Everything should have been as new and strange as what had just happened. But the dusty trees stood silent against the tin sky, and below, in the distance, Atlanta's mirrored buildings still captured the sun and burned. Then the word *dead* amazed her, the way it came out of her mouth as though she said it every day of her life. "Well, that's what they tell me," she said to Mae Ruth as her sister sat there, hands gripping the steering wheel, exactly the way she'd been caught when Ruby dropped the word onto her up-turned face. Then she was surprised by her sister's voice, how it boiled on and on shaped like questions, while Ruby breathed easily, lightheaded as a little seed carried on the wind. It was the most natural thing in the world that Beau should be dead; it had never been any other way. She patted her sister's hand: "That sneaky little thing just slipped right out on me," she said, chuckling to herself and wiping her eyes with the backs of both hands. And her heart gave a surge and pushed the next wave of words out, as though she were speaking to Beau himself, come back from the dead to taunt her: "That sneaky little bastard," she said, "goddamn him."

Mae Ruth drove like a crazy woman — running red lights, laying on the horn, heading back toward Cotton Bottom at sixty miles an hour, gripping Ruby's wrist with one hand. "We got to get you home," she said.

"You do that," Ruby said. It would be nice to be back there among the skinny houses that bunched so close together you could hear your neighbor drop a spoon. She could slip in there like somebody's ghost and nobody'd find her again. That was the comfort of the village — the tight fit made people invisible. Too many people with too much trouble lived here, and everybody had gotten in the habit of going around deaf and blind just so they could have some peace now and again. She could hide there and never come out again, the way Old Lady Steel did after her kid got run over by a drunk: rocking on her porch day and night, cringing anytime tires squealed, and crying out at the sight of children in the street. That was a good use for life, she thought. She just might take it up like so many of the rest of her neighbors. They saw something once, something horrible, and it stuck to their eyes and the look of it never left them.

When they turned onto Rhineheart Street, Ruby sat up.

"This ain't right, Mae Ruth, you took a wrong turn some-where," she said anxiously. Her gaze never left the road that ran into a lake of white light, a mirage. In the glare, her street looked like a familiar place that had been warped. Then there was her house and the neighbors three deep on the narrow porch because somehow the news had gotten loose and run home before her. And she saw that the glare, the mirage, was a trick of the light on the windshield and she sat back and said, "Oh, now I get it. Fools you, don't it?" And she chuckled to herself. Someone had played a fine joke and now it was revealed.

The place where Ruby lives is called Cotton Bottom be-cause of the cotton mill and because it's set in a low spot, a slump in the earth. The streets there run straight between the mill on one end of the place and the vacated company store on the other. In February when the weather settles in and the rain falls straight down, the air turns gray and thin, and there's silence as though the air had all been sucked into the big whistle on top of the mill and scattered again to the four corners of the earth. But in the summer, this place comes alive: the kids all go around beating on garbage-can lids, the air is so full of their noise you couldn't lose them if you tried, and the heat is so heavy you drag it with you from place to place.

The other border of this place is an old city cemetery with a pauper's field of unmarked graves on a low hill. Ruby used to go there between shifts or after work if it was still light and sit and listen to the wind roughing up the tops of the trees. They were the biggest trees she'd ever seen – oaks, some with crowns as wide as rooftops. Sometimes she thought of the roots of the trees, and it gave her

7

a funny cold knot in the pit of her stomach to think of the roots and the bodies down there all mixed up together, the bones in among the roots, feeding the trees. She sat very quietly then, listening, as if she might catch that long story as it begins below the ground, as it rises and ends in the wind, in the tossing crowns of the oaks, in the way they sigh and bend and rise and lash the air again.

By eight o'clock the morning after Beau's death the sun looked brassy, as though it had burned all day. You had to breathe in small sips for fear you'd suck in too much heat and choke on it. Everybody was busy mopping at themselves, blotting their upper lips, women reaching back, lifting their hair and fanning their necks. Ruby didn't question how the night had passed; she watched while the sweating men struggled and pushed Beau's coffin up the narrow steps. And as she watched them coming closer she had one of her thoughts that seemed to come out of nowhere: Who is that stranger coming here?

She must have mumbled it to herself, because Dan Malvern and Mae Ruth both leaned over at the same time to catch what she'd said. "You'd think that'd be the easy part," she said, nodding toward the men with the coffin. Her arms hung at her sides; her face was slack, red and chafed-looking; her feet were planted wide to keep her upright. When they passed with Beau's coffin, her mouth went dry and her knees gave a little and Dan squeezed her arm and whispered: "Ruby, you hold on now." His warm breath on her ear annoyed her.

She tried not to listen to the rustling of the undertakers, the way they whispered as they fussed with the casket.

They opened the casket and draped an organdy net from the lid to the floor and arranged it in a pool around the legs of the coffin stand and it all seemed to be happening beyond glass somewhere. The open lid was lined with shirred white satin – the richest cloth she'd ever been close to, that was for sure – gathered into a sunburst. Below it her son rested on his cushions with that stubborn look stuck to his face as though he were about to say *No* the way he did: jutting out his chin and freezing his eyes and defying the world to say him *Yes*. "I never believed it," she said, and the words were cold drops in her ears, "not for a minute, and now look." And with that, a heaviness in her chest dragged on her, she turned on the people close by and said: "What was the way he should've come, tell me that? What other road could he have gone, why doesn't somebody tell me?" She grabbed Mae Ruth's arm.

"Be strong, darlin'," Mae Ruth said, from somewhere close beside her ear. "You got to be strong now."

She sank into the chair they had guided her to. It seemed that she'd been strong forever and in everything. Just after Beau was born sick she'd been strong in her faith. It had leapt on her one day like something that had been lying in wait getting ready. Afterwards, she'd gone about preaching the Word to anyone who'd stand still long enough to hear. That's when Charles Clinton had left for the first time. But the Lord had stayed, yes He had. He sent His mighty spirit down to fill her where she stood inside the Holiness Lighthouse Tabernacle over on Gaskill Street. He slung her onto the floor and filled her some more till she was so full of His spirit it pressed out against the walls of her chest, the walls of her skull, till she thought it might tear her open, trying to get free. She'd swooped down on her neighbor's houses after that night – praying, singing, weeping for all who lived there sunk in the sin and error of their ways, their sin a pressure building inside her as if it were her sin too. On Sunday, she sang the hymns with the force and flatness of a hammer hitting a rock, and on Wednesday evenings at prayer meeting, she beat the tambourine so hard that no one could stand close to her.

Then she'd been strong at work in the mill. First, she wielded the sharp razor, slashed open the bails so the cotton tumbled out. She roughed up the cotton and set it going toward the other room to be wooed and combed straight into fiber. They took note of how she worked and she was promoted to spooler. She stood beside the machines until she thought the veins in her legs might burst. She worked there yanking levers, guiding the threads as they sped along from one spool to the next. You had to yank the levers because the machines were old and balky, but the habit of it became the same as its action and the habit felt like fury after awhile. The threads flew by, never slowing, drawing tighter, flying from one spool to the next, the separate strands twisting, making miles of continuous threads for the big looms in the room beyond. The noise could deafen a person. The machines reared up and fell forward in unison and grabbed the fiber with metal claws and twisted the strands and rose and grabbed and fell again in rhythm all day and all night. The machines crashed like sacks full of silver being dropped again and again until she couldn't think, she could only watch the threads as they came flying out of the dark door and caught and flashed around the spools and flew out the other door.

For years she went to work during the day and at night she went to prayer meetings or to church singings. Later, when the Lord had eased up on her, she'd been with a bunch of women praying together one night when something ugly had come into their midst, something that smelled like burnt hair, and she'd stepped to the front like she knew just what to do. She'd been strong for them all and she'd led them in raising their voices louder in God's praise, every fiber set against the thing that had entered and filled the room right in the middle of prayer. She'd known right away that whatever it might be, it was between this thing and Beau that she needed to stand. "Don't be afraid," she said. She made *quiet down* motions with her hands and she said: "You know, it comes to me to say there isn't nothing strange under the sun, not good and not bad either one. There is this thing we call the Devil and that old Devil turns things inside out and upside-down just that quick. Why, he spins you around and turns you around and scares you into thinking that he's stronger than anything you can call on, ain't that right?" And that, she told them, was the work this Devil was appointed to do on this earth.

But the work didn't stop there, oh no. The work went on working and people began to call themselves shameful and ugly before God. You could see it all the time, she told them, in the sad empty eyes around you. And the end of the work came when people turned into living tombstones over their own lives, when people hid their faces from one another; then the work was finished, she told them. "Now you've all seen it happen," she said. "Every single one of us in this room's seen it happen. But the way I figure it, we got to go one better than that. We got to stand up and say 'All right then, I got something for you better than what you got for me." That's what we're all put here to do on this earth, and we can't ever let each other forget."

But that all seemed to have happened in another lifetime, in another country, a long time ago. Now there was this: the undertakers finished their business and left the house. Ruby dragged the reclining chair right next to the steel-gray coffin and eased herself down, feeling like a bag of flesh with a cold stone at the center. The coffin looked cold and shiny as coins, and her mind wandered there, counting the coins.

The green vinyl of the chair arms stuck to the back of her arms, and she saw the looks go around the room from Mae Ruth to her aunts, to Granny Brassler and the rest of them. Looks and sighs that flew around the room, passing from one to another, but she didn't care. She knew what they were thinking; she'd thought the same herself many a time about someone else: they were worrying that all the fight had gone out of her and wondering what they would do with another one to feed and wipe clean. In the village, that's the worst that can happen. "I'm here to stay," she said, "don't want no bath, don't want no supper, so don't start on me about it, just tend to your business and let me tend to mine."

She thought of that business and how she'd learned it well. To work, to live you had to be angry, you had to fight – that much she remembered. Her father had fought for his life, for all their lives, the time half the mill walked out, and the mill police came muscling into their house on fat horses.

She could still see the door frame give, see her father's arm raised, all the veins standing up, before he brought the stick of stove wood down hard across the horse's nose. That was what life was for — fighting to keep it. That's how she'd been raised. All the good sweet passion and flavor of life soured if you just let it sit. Like milk left out, it could spoil. You had to be strong.

She smelled her own exhausted smell, like old iron, leaving her. Someone had drawn the curtains across the front window. Someone wiped her face with a cloth. They bent over her one after the other. "Ruby, trust in the Lord," someone said. The thought rolled over her.

"I do," she said automatically, because the Lord was still a fact, more or less. "But it's got nothing to do with him." She nodded toward her son. There. She was afraid to say it, but that was the truth. She snapped up straight, defying any of them to say differently. And just then she was taken by grief that pushed up in waves from the dead center of her. Each wave lifted her out of the chair and wrenched her voice from her throat, and that voice warned them: "I can't bear it." She couldn't open her eyes and inside the darkness there was a darker darkness, a weight like a ball, rolling against the back of her eyes. "I can't support it," she said and everything obliged inside her and fell in, and there was a quick glimpse of Beau the way he'd come home one time after a fight — tatters of blood in the sink, too much blood to be coming out of his nose and no way to stop it — and she was falling, tumbling over and over. Someone shouted her name; hands held her face, her hands. They bobbed all around her, corks on a dark water.

And when finally she opened her eyes, she glared at them

as if they'd waked her from a deep sleep. She looked at Beau's face: they had messed with it somehow till it looked almost rosy, and chalky too, dusted with powder. His hair was washed straight back as though a wave had combed it, so silky and fine. He'd taken to dyeing his hair – the roots were dark and a soapy cloying smell rose through the organdy – and she said on the last receding wave of grief: "Lord, don't I wonder what's keeping him company right now."

"Now don't you go wandering off there all by yourself," Mae Ruth said. Her eyes were inches from Ruby's own. Ruby looked at her sister and almost laughed in spite of herself at the funny veiny nose, more like a beak than a nose, the eyes like her own, two flat dark buttons. Now Mae Ruth's life was hard too, but it didn't fit her so tight. She made room in it. She could tell funny stories, then turn around and tell somebody off just as neat and they'd stay told off. Once they'd both gone to a palm reader out by Doraville and the woman had scared Ruby, and Mae Ruth had said, "Lady, far's I'm concerned you get your jollies out of scaring people half to death." That was Mae Ruth for you. Just then her face looked like she was about to imitate the way the woman had looked. Mae Ruth could pull her face down long as a hound's and say "Doom" in this deep funny voice and you'd have to laugh.

Someone new had come into the room. She felt it in the stirring among the crowd around her chair, the way they coughed and got quiet. "Dan?" she said. He'd left the room after the coffin was carried inside and had gone to stand outside with the men on the porch. She looked up, expecting to find Dan's narrow brown face, and there stood Charles

Clinton and his new wife, looking cool in spite of the heat. "Well, look who's here," she said, "look who's showing his face around here again." The welcome in her voice would have chilled you to the bone. "Look who's come back to the well," she said. "Well's dried up, Charles Clinton," she said. Her breathing turned down like a low gas flame. His new wife tried to get in her line of vision, but Ruby kept ducking around her in order to keep an eye fixed on Charles. And doesn't it always happen this way? When she was most in need of the mercy of forgetfulness – just then, she remembered everything.

She was sixteen, up from Atlanta to Gainesville for the Chicopee Mill picnic. He stood apart from everybody, working a stick of gum, his eyes all over her every time she moved. The lights inside the mill had come winging out through the hundreds of small windows. Like stars, they'd winked on the water of the millpond. And the roaring of the mill barely reached them across the mild night, and it was no longer noise that could make you deaf. The air was clean of cotton lint and clear, and the mill glittered. Everything glittered that way. Oh yes, she remembered that glittering very well. He had eyes like dry ice. She should have known; she should have turned and run with what she knew instead of thinking she could sass and sharp-tongue her way out of everything. He said: "You're Ruby Nelson from Atlanta, aren't you?"

"How'd you know?" she said.

"I have my ways," he said. And thinking about those ways had made her shiver.

She should have bolted for sure. She was supposed to have married Hudger Collins, and she had no business forgetting that. But Hudger was dull next to this one who had hair like corn silk, a sloped and angled face that reminded her of an Indian, and slanted eyes that watched and watched.

"I take you for a soldier," she said. And he smiled that smile that rippled out across his face and was gone so fast you couldn't catch it.

"Now you're a right smart girl," he said, wrapping one hand around the top of her arm. "It just so happens that I was in the Navy. You're real smart."

Later that night as they lay over near the edge of the woods where the grass was dry and patchy, he said her name again and again as if he wanted to drive it into her. Now when she saw him again a pit opened inside her and all the fiends let fly. She looked at Beau jealously, as if he might rise up and join his father and together they'd waltz away into the night. She said: "Charles Clinton, why don't you come over here and look at your boy. He's dead, he isn't going to get up and worry you now. You don't have nothing to be ashamed of anymore." She hated her voice when it got quavery like that. She heard a dry crackling sob burst out of Charles's throat and nose and she leaned her head back and smiled at the ceiling. "Why don't you come closer," she said. "You know me and him both." She patted the edge of the coffin.

"Ruby," Mae Ruth rasped in her ear, "everyone's suffering, let him be."

Ruby hooted and smacked the arm of the chair. "Who's suffering?" she said. "How can you tell when Charles Clinton's suffering?"

"Oh Lord," someone said from the corner of the room, "there's just no end to it."

He stepped closer, and for the first time she looked directly into his eyes. She was afraid to do it because she believed in what she saw in people's eyes. Halfway into another bitter word she saw his eyes and bit her lip. His eyes were washed out, drained, the color broken. His mouth turned down, and something elastic was gone from under his skin. He'd lost a tooth, and though his powder-blue leisure suit was clean, the backs of his knuckles looked grimy, like soot had been rubbed in under his skin. And those were the very eyes I searched and searched, she thought, the ones where I tried to see myself for so long. And those eyes stared at her, void of anything but a steady pain that threatened to break from him. It scared her so much she couldn't speak, and she leaned over and fussed with the net over Beau's coffin.

She didn't love Charles, never had, she'd known that from the start. But it acted like love, like a horse colt kicking inside her whenever he laid her down. And it was time – Ruby saw that in men's eyes when she passed them by on the street, and she saw it in her mother's eyes – time to start that kind of living and hope that she came to love him down the road. Hope that they'd come to be like Pappy and Mama had been before they'd moved to Atlanta to work in the mill, standing together in the field with their long burlap cotton sacks trailing behind them, picking cotton together and filling those sacks till the whole length of them was stuffed with their time together. That's what she'd seen could come of a married life. That's what she'd believed.

She wore a tight dress of lilac-colored imitation linen all the way to Jacksonville on the bus. It was their honeymoon trip, but all the while she had the sense that she was riding along beside herself. Away over there was the girl who was wild crazy in love, but she, Ruby, couldn't get to her. All the while she waited for the special feeling to come up in her throat, the way a spring starts up out of the ground. She wanted that feeling, but it didn't come. She didn't love him, but she shut that knowledge away. That was her secret. She always believed it would be different, and that was her secret. And her faith, and her shame.

So, love or no love, and faithful to another law, Beau was born barely moving, hardly breathing. His lips stayed blue for the longest time. And both times — after the birth when the doctor had come in peeling off his rubber gloves, talking about some little something in Beau's heart that wouldn't close right, and now — Charles had stood there looking like something broken, his face taking on no more expression than the dead boy's. Only his eyes still spoke, and his hand trembled like an old man's hand as he lifted it to wipe his mouth. Why, I'm better off than he is, she thought. For all this, I'm better off. It was cold, proud comfort. The sweet vengeful cry she'd hoped for, the bass string she'd hoped to hear singing inside her at the sight of him broken by the death of his only son, wouldn't sound. She grabbed for Mae Ruth's hand because the falling sensation was creeping in behind her eyes again.

The fact of the boy had stuck in Charles like a bone in his throat. She spent her days sitting in the Grady Hospital clinics with Beau's heavy head lolling over one arm, because there had to be an answer. You'd have thought the boy was contaminated the way Charles's hands had stiffened when he picked up the baby. You'd have thought the boy was permanently crippled or contagious the way he held him away from his body. "Lots and lots of people's born with something just a little off," she said. "Lord, some of them never even know it," she told Charles pointedly. Of course, as things had gone on, the depth of the damage had been revealed, as it always is. By the time Beau had surgery on his heart at the age of five, Charles wouldn't even come up to sit with him. He said it was too humiliating to sit in the charity ward, where people treated you like you were something to be mopped off the floor.

And after Beau had managed to grow up and after he started coming home with pockets full of dollar bills, Charles could only say "What's going on?" She could almost see the words forming on his lips as he looked at his son in the coffin. Charles never understood a thing; that was his sorrow. She didn't want him near her.

She remembered her own sorrow, how it had struck so deep it had seemed to disappear inside her the first time Beau got caught in Grant Park in a car with a rich man from the north side of town. He was nothing but a baby, twelve years old. The police cruiser brought him home because the other man was not only rich, he was also important, and he didn't want trouble on account of Beau. Her son smelled like baby powder and dirty clothes. He was growing a face to hide behind. His lips were swollen as though someone had been kissing them too hard, and she stared and wondered whether that brand was put on his mouth by love or by hate or by some other force too strange to be named. She had to drag Charles into the room. "It ain't the money," Charles had shrieked at his son. "I know it ain't just for money." That was as much of the discovery as he could force out of his mouth; the rest was too terrifying.

"Why?" she asked her son. Her voice bored into him. She held onto his skinny arm and watched the skin blanch under her fingers.

"They talk nice to me," Beau said.

"Honey, those men don't care about you," she said, watching Charles turn away, watching Beau watch him turn away.

When Charles left, he said their life wasn't fit for human beings, and he moved out to Chamblee. He'd never lifted a hand against her. By Cotton Bottom standards that made him a good man. But she felt that violence had been done to her; there was a hardness and a deadness inside that made her swerve away from people as though she might catch something from them.

During that time, she went to Dan Malvern. It was right: he was her pastor as well as her friend, and together they'd puzzled over that deadness and prayed endlessly for forgiveness for her. She was never quite sure for what sin she needed to be forgiven, but she'd kept quiet and prayed anyway.

Now, sitting beside Beau's coffin, she'd come a whole revolution: she felt like asking for forgiveness about as much as she felt like getting up and walking to New York City. Forgiveness belonged to another lifetime, to people like Dan who had a vision left to guide them. Once, Dan had seen armies of souls pouring toward heaven and hell while he stood at the crossroads, frantically directing traffic. From that day on, he said, his cross and burden was to stand there until the Lord called him home. Now Dan stood just outside the door with his big black shoes sticking out of his too-short pants. You had to be gentle with Dan; he always had to be invited, so she said: "Dan'l, you're always welcome here." He crossed the room with one long country stride and grabbed her hand and rubbed it and said: "Are you holding up all right in the care of the Lord?"

"Getting by," she said. His eyes looked old. She took his hand more warmly and said: "Dan, bless you." But when she took her hand away it hung in front of her, bare and powerless. And there was Beau, dead, his life full of violence in spite of that hand, and she said "Oh," and bit her knuckle. Dan hauled her up, pulled her into the kitchen, and shut the door behind him. He rested a hand on her shoulder and threw back his head, and the tears squeezed out through the lashes like beads. She moved to embrace him but he stopped her. He was maneuvering into the current, setting his back to the wind. He shifted and hunched his shoulders: "Kneel down with me, sister," he said.

"Oh, all right, Dan," she said, sighing. She knew this part of the ritual, when they had to forget each other's names in order that God might hear their prayers. She knelt down facing him. She had to endure this because when Dan wasn't busy acting like God's own special riding-mule, he was one who shed a steady light onto her life, a light in which she could stand holding her shame and be loved, shame and all. Mae Ruth was another, only her light was barer and warmer. Dan remembered her and could remind her sometimes of ways she'd been that she could hardly recall. He knew her practically all the way back. She could go to him feeling small and cold, the way lights look in winter, and come away after talking about nothing for a few hours, with her feet set squarely on this earth again.

But something happened when he talked about God,

when he started to pray. They didn't have much in common then. He became hard, he saw things in black and white and spoke of them harshly through his gritted teeth. His jawbone tried to pop through the skin, and his black hair began to tremble with indignation, and he jerked at the words as if he were chewing stringy meat. He strained after the words as though he could pull them from the air: "Lord, help her to see that sin is there," he began, "that sin has taken away her son. Help her to see the sin, to look on the *wages* of sin and to ask forgiveness, and help this woman, your servant, to know in her HEART the sin and to call OUT to the Lord in her hour of need."

She would have laughed had she not felt so lonely. Dan could let himself down into it anytime and drink of the stern comfort there. She envied him that plunge. She imagined that the relief must taste hard and clean as water from a deep well sunk through rock. She closed her eyes and tried to pray, to sink into that place. It would be so good to believe again in the laws, she thought, because those laws named the exile and the means of coming home in such clear ringing tones. First there was sin, a person drifting in some foreign land, then confessing the sin, then redemption, then hallelujah, sister, and welcome home. She felt for her heart, for its secret shame, and found only a sort of homesickness, a notion that there was some place that she'd forgotten, a place where there were no such people as foreigners, a place big enough to hold sin, grief, ugliness, all of it.

But forgetfulness, that was the sickness, the worm in the heart. Words like *good* and *evil* and *death* simplified things and rocked you and lulled you and split things apart. There was something else moving back there; she could barely feel it but it was there.

She watched his face move through the prayer, laboring against a current, and when he came back to himself with a great bass "Amen" she said "Amen" too, and a sob broke from her at the sound of that blank word. Her shoulders shook and her head wagged from side to side and she said: "Dan, I'm gonna tell you something. It must tire out the Lord himself to listen to all that talk about sin all the time. There must be some wages due to you for that, wouldn't you say?"

"Ruby," he said, "don't blaspheme now, don't go piling sin on sin."

At that, she labored to her feet and shook herself. "The way I understand it," she said, "we're all born fools, ain't that right? Nothing we can do about that. What's the sin in that? Seems like everything we do has got wages." The man of God with thunder and sword faded, and his face was restored to him, and the Daniel she knew came back, looking sheepish, pulling on his bottom lip. "So where are you going to look for better wages is what I want to know?"

"I know you're under a terrible strain," he said, "but I don't know where you get such talk." But by then she was halfway into the other room. And seeing her son in his coffin again, she felt she was coming on him fresh, and she saw how much Beau's face looked like her own – much more like her own than like Charles's face – and it scared her. The life he'd led showed in the set defiance of the chin, in the squint-marks around the eyes that the mortician's powder puff couldn't erase. That look was stuck there for all eternity, and he was only sixteen years old.

It was the same look he'd given her anytime she'd asked him about those men and why he went with them. She'd fought for him for so long and the fatigue of that fight caught up with her again and she was tossed up on a fresh wave of grief. She began to sob and twist, turning this way and that, trying to escape from the people who pressed in from all sides, suffocating her. Strong hands gripped her and shook her, and she recognized Dan and Mae Ruth, though neither of them spoke and her eyes were squeezed tight. "Get it out," Mae Ruth said. "You go on and get it all out, then you come on back here with us."

"I think I want to sleep for awhile now," she said, opening her eyes.

"You want a nerve pill?" Mae Ruth asked. She shook her head. She stopped beside the coffin.

"Well now," she said softly, "don't he look sweeter without that harsh light on him?" During the minute that she'd had her spell of grief, the light had shifted, softened to gray, pressing in at the windows. As the light softened in the room, her son's face softened too; he looked younger and not so angry at the air. He hadn't looked that way since he was a baby, and she loved him with a sweetness so sharp she felt she might be opened by it.

And what became of that sweetness, she wondered, as she pushed through the curtains into her bedroom. By what devilish sly paths did it run away, leaving the harsh light that never ceased burning on him? It took too much effort to remember that he was not just that strange being who'd thrashed his way through her life and out, leaving wreckage in his path. He was also another thing, but it made her head hurt to think of it. She pulled off her slippers and unhooked her slacks at the waist. It was easier to think that the march he'd made straight to his grave was the sin, to call that life ugly and be done with it. But the changing of the sweet to the ugly was the most obvious trick in the book. Anyone with eyes could see through that one. There was a better trick. She thought how much she wished she could still believe that the Devil dreamed up the tricks. That would explain the ashes around her heart.

But never mind: the better trick was that the soft curtains of forgetfulness dropped so quietly you did not hear them fall. It was forgetfulness that made things and people seem strange: that was sin if ever there was sin. Still, remembering things made you so tired. Better to live blind, she thought.

Once she'd begged Beau to remember who he was. She'd meant *her* people, the Nelson side, dignity and decency deep enough to last through two or three lifetimes. But they were as strange to him as the whole rest of the wide world. "Sure," he'd said, "I know who I am. I'm a Nelson from the cotton patch and a Clinton straight from hell." Seeing her shocked, with her hand pressed to her throat, he'd laughed and said: "Well ain't I? You're always saying 'Goddamn your daddy to hell.'" The way he'd imitated her, his mouth drawn back like a wild animal's, had terrified her. "That means I come from hell, don't it, Mama?"

She shook her head in frustration and eased herself down onto her bed. She wished that he were there, given back to her for just one minute, so that she could collect, finally, all she'd needed to tell him, so that she could tell him in words he'd have to understand, that if one person loved you, you were not a chunk of dead rock spinning in space. That was what she'd tried to tell him all during the long winter just past.

That was the winter when the mill had stepped up production again and had taken on everyone they'd laid off. She'd gotten a job in the sewing room. All day she sat there sewing, while her mind worked to find an end to the business with Beau. It was quieter there than in the weave room and she could forget about everything but one seam running under her needle, one train of thought going through her mind. Last winter he was gone more than he was home, and his face was pale and sunken around the cheekbones. Every so often she'd start way back at the beginning and come forward with him step by step, puzzling out the way and ending always in the same spot: the place she'd seen him staring into. She turned it over and over like the piecework in front of her, looking for the bunched thread, the too-long stitch that would give, the place where her mind had wandered and the machine had wandered off the seam.

Once she'd taken half a sick-day and had gone home to find him staring at nothing. She'd barely been able to rouse him, and when she'd bent over him she'd been repelled by his sweet sick odor. But it was the way he'd looked that stuck in her mind: tight blue jeans, a black shirt, a red bandanna wound tightly around his neck. And his face, when he'd finally turned it up to her and smiled dreamily into her screaming, was sly and serene as the face of a wrecked angel. It was the smile that made her blood shut off. When he smiled that way, there was a shudder in the room like the sound that lingered in the air if the looms shut down, and she knew that he was bound to die, that he was already looking into that place. She saw it in his eyes all winter.

The cotton came in bailed through enormous doors and was pulped, twisted, spun, woven, mixed with polyester and squeezed and pressed and dyed and made into sheets and blouses and printed with tulips, irises, gardens of blowing green.

It wasn't right that she should worry herself the way she did all winter. She was up all hours of the night waiting for him, but half the time he never came home. Then one day she just went into his room and nailed the window shut, and when he went into his room that night, she locked him in and sat in the living room with arms folded, crying, as he bumped and crashed around and screamed awful names at her. It was for his own good and because she loved him. And if you loved somebody, she told herself, you had to make a stand and this was her stand. In the morning she'd explain to him, in words he'd have to understand, that she did it out of love.

Afterwards she was ashamed, and she never told anyone, not even Mae Ruth. She felt that she'd been in a dream, a fever dream, where crazy things made perfect sense and everything hung suspended way up high in clear air. But it didn't matter anyway because when she unlocked the door to set him free in the morning, he was gone. Glass all over the floor and the window kicked out.

She woke up after dark, groping around with one hand, looking for something on the bedspread. She'd been dreaming of black rocks looming over her, and at the base of the rocks, hundreds of people scrambling around, picking up busted-off pieces of the largest rock and holding them up in the moonlight. She groped her way out into the living room, and people patted her and helped her ease down into her chair again.

All night she slept and woke. Whenever she woke, one pair of hands or another reached for her, and once she tried to say: "I want to thank you all for being so good." But her voice broke when she said "good," and someone said: "Hush, you'd do the same."

The voices went round and round her, a soothing drone that filled the room. Then the sun was up, the day was up bright and blazing. She looked at her son beside her in his coffin, and the thought of his going broke over her like a wave. And as the day rushed back at her, so did her memories of Beau, which were as sharp as if he were still alive. In fact, they were hardly memories at all, they were more like the small sightings we keep of someone's day-to-day life.

This is how he came in: her body had threshed with him for two days and a night. Then his sickness: she walked him day and night, while over on Tye Street Granny Brassler and the others went down almost to their knees, taken by the spirit, shouting: "Devil, take your hands off that baby."

He was never full of milk and quiet; he was long and gangly and he never fleshed out. And all the while he was growing a man's mind. By the time he was twelve, right after Charles left, he'd stay gone for days, nobody knew where. Then, last June, he and his friends had started sticking closer to home, robbing the men in the park nearby. That's when she'd set herself against him in earnest. The last time she'd smacked him good had been right there in the kitchen just as she was setting supper down on the table, when he'd come busting through the door yelling how someone was a nigger motherfucker. She'd grabbed his face and squeezed and said: "Don't you never let me hear you talking like trash again. You are not and never will be trash, and don't you forget it."

"Everybody calls me trash," he said. "What makes you any different?"

"Cause I'm your people," she said. "Cause you're mine."

"Ain't that funny?" he said. "That's what they say too."

Every time, somebody else was holding the gun, but the next time, or the time after that, she knew it would be Beau, and then he would be tried as an adult and sent away to the real prison up at Alto, and that would be that. Last June they'd only taken him as far as the jumping-off place, the *juvenile evaluation center* they called it. But it was a prison as surely as Alto where he'd end up someday, looking out with the others at the blue mountains beyond the high wire fence.

She wasn't like the other mothers, the ones who wept or pleaded or shouted. That time was long gone, and she knew it. She was there for another reason but it had no name, only a glare, like the harsh sunlight on the white white walls of his room. She listened. He beat time on his thigh with the heel of one hand and talked, and sometimes he looked up and said: "Ain't that right?" And with knees spread, elbows resting on her knees, hands loosely knotted and fallen between her knees, she looked back at him and said: "No, that isn't right Beau, not as I see it," in the strongest voice she could muster.

Staying, listening and staying, was a habit she'd had to learn. The first visit to the evaluation center had ended with her reeling out of the room, driven back by his words that were so ugly they seemed to coil like tar snakes out of his mouth. But she went back, *she did go back*, and she knew she must never let herself forget that. She went back and she listened to every word, and she had never felt so empty, so silent. The city, the room turned strange around her, and the only familiar face was the one just in front of her, the one with the mouth that opened and said: "You ought to see their faces when Roy shows them the gun."

She looked up quickly, hearing that voice again just as clear as if it were still ringing off the walls of the jail. She looked at his dead face, and her head began to tug with it, and she stood and bore down on him while all around her the dark closed in as it does when a person's about to faint. Only she was far from fainting. The dark narrowed around her until she stood inside a dark egg looking down at her son, the stranger made up for his grave, who rested in a wash of light that lingered at the core of the outer dark shell. And as she watched and listened – watching and listening with every cell – the stranger's face dropped away and the whole harsh chorus of his life tangled in her and sang again, and she remembered what she'd seen in the jail, what she'd seen a long time before the jail and had forgotten and carried with her the whole stubborn way and had never wanted to believe, and had believed: he was lost, and he had always been lost. His hands were folded, his face eternally still. Whatever he had been, he was now, forever. She gripped the coffin's edge while the fury rose up her legs and belly and chest and gathered inside her skull, a familiar pressure, and she wanted to strike or curse someone over what had become of this child. From the moment he was born, he was lost, *her own child*, lost. For a long time she'd believed that he was two children: one hers, the other possessed by another power. All his life, she'd worked to pull or wrestle *her* child free from the hold of his lost brother, to love the one, rage against the other and drive him out. She touched the wing of his nose where it flared out so pretty, then pulled her fingers away quickly and slipped her hand into the pocket of her dress. But it was too late. When she touched his skin, everything collapsed and ran together again, and there was no such thing as love apart from rage or this child freed from his own lost self. Nothing could be untangled, nothing pulled apart. Not then. Not now. Not ever. The roots all went down deep – the root of love, the root of fury, the root of the child – like the roots of the oaks that grew on the hill in the old cemetery on the border of this place. Down they went, and down, and mixed with the bones until the bones were roots and the roots, bones, and the trees grew tall over everything.

She stood very still, looking at his pinched white face. For the first time, she understood a Bible verse that people had always quoted at her. Dan had used it, everybody used it to tell her how to feel about trouble but she, Ruby, understood it for herself now, and no one could take it from her. *I will lift up mine eyes to the hills*, she thought. She looked and she saw the crowns of the oaks brushing the sky, and below the trees she saw the tangled maze of roots running through the hill of the dead. That was all the comfort there was.

She sat down in her chair with a moan and began to rock herself and to pat the edge of the coffin in time with her rocking. She saw the panic start up on every face, and she pressed a hand to her chest to quiet herself. "Things should slow down," she said, "so that a person can have time to study them."

As though they'd been held back, people crowded into the room again. The air got sticky and close, and the smell of flowers and sweat and not quite clean clothes and the soapy smell that hung over Beau's coffin began to make her dizzy. So she focused on Charles and a prickly rash began to spread over her neck and arms and her vision began to clear. Finally she said, in a lazy kind of voice – lazy like a cottonmouth moccasin stirring the water – "Charles, you and your wife's taking up more than your share of the air in here. Why don't you just step out onto the porch?" They ignored her. But Mae Ruth clucked her tongue.

"Ruby, shame, he's still the boy's father; you can't deny him that," she said.

"I know that," Ruby snapped. "Don't I wish I didn't."

She closed her eyes and wished for the old way, the old law that said *the ones that give, get back in kind*. She wished that the weight of that law might lie in her hand like a rock. She wished for some revenge sweet enough to fit his crimes, the kind of revenge that came from a time before people were condemned to stand linked to one another. She could make him order the tombstone and have Beau's name drilled there, yes, and be gone before the funeral started. She tried it out on herself but the little cold thrill the thought gave her wasn't enough to satisfy. Oh me, she said to herself, there isn't no country far enough away where I could send him. She opened her eyes and searched the room for a single unfamiliar face on which to rest her eyes, and found not a one. And she felt the whole dense web of love and grief descending, settling over her shoulders as it had before, in the prison. "This don't ever stop," she said out loud. And she thought of how she had never loved Charles, not in the way that a woman loves a man, and how, still, he was part of the law that turned and turned and bound them all together, on each turn, more closely than before.

Then there was the vault out under the strong sun without a tent to cover it, and the flowers were wilting under the sun, and Mae Ruth's strong voice led off a song. Then Daniel spoke of dust, and of heaven and the Redeemer for a long time. They were in a new cemetery and the lots were parceled out of a flat field. Through the thin soles of her shoes, Ruby could feel the rucks and ripples of once-plowed ground. She wore a dress of hard black cloth that trapped the heat inside and made the sweat trickle down her sides. Charles stood on the edge of the crowd, his chin sunk onto his chest, and he looked faded under the light that seemed to gather into a center that was made of even whiter and hotter light.

Ruby barely listened to the resurrection and the life. She saw her son's face: surrounded by darkness now, closed in darkness forever. Those words Dan said, they weren't the prayers, she thought, not the real prayers. The prayer rested in the coffin, in the dark there. Her eyes followed its deaf, dumb lines. The prayer was his life that she couldn't save, and the prayer was her own life and how it continued. And the prayer never stopped; lives began and ended, but the prayer never stopped. She looked at the ground and had the sensation that she'd been standing there for a very long time, trying to memorize each one of the scrappy weeds that had begun to grow again out of the plowed-over land. Those weeds were like the threads; she watched them in the same way. The threads flew toward her like slender rays of light and twisted spool to spool and disappeared through another door toward the looms beyond. The sound of their coming and going made one continuous roar.

Because she wanted it that way, they all stayed as the coffin was lowered into the hole. She stepped up to the side of the grave and saw her own shadow, thrown huge, on the lid of the vault. It startled her so much she stepped forward instead of back and the edges crumbled under her shoes. Then there were hands on her arms, and she looked down again and saw Mae Ruth's shadow and Dan's beside her. It was as though they were in a boat together, looking over the side. And the sun beat down on them all: on the living, and into the grave, and on those who had lived and died.

World of Women

IN THE WATER with Sara, he knows how clumsy he is, how small. As they stand waist-deep in the pool and he tries once again to tell her what frightens him so about swimming, he feels himself becoming transparent under her stare, colorless as the water she scoops as she listens, thin as the same water trickling between her fingers. His face heats up and to cool it he holds his nose, ducks, waits for Sara's hand to grope after him, to drag him back to the surface. These days even a good ducking doesn't work. When he comes up he's still small, bewildered and red-faced as a baby, as though the water had washed away the boy he thought he knew, the one who was becoming a little mysterious and complicated, more like a maze than a straight line, and given him back this helpless, colorless boy who chokes at the thought of swimming. Meanwhile, Sara listens and looks clear through him with her keen green eyes and he wishes he could snap his fingers, *vamoose* as the cowboys say, and wake up back in his room at home, miles and years from this water. But he is not at home, not in his room or his bed; he is at the city pool with Sara, learning to swim while people yell and splash, agitating the water into sharp blue peaks that slap against his stomach. He shivers and waits for this lesson to be over, following the sound of her voice, hugging himself and waiting for the bliss of Sara's thick blue towel to descend and wrap him, for Sara's hand to lead him out of the pool.

Sara's connected in some way with the university downtown where Mark's father teaches and his mother works. Sara's much younger than his mother; Mark and his brother Peter used to spy on her through the banister rails around the landing that overlooks their entrance hall. Sara usually came alone; she wore her hair in two braids crossed over the back of her head and sometimes when she shrugged off her coat, Mark glimpsed her shoulder before she pulled her blouse straight. But once she came with a man, a person who smoked cigarettes and wore galoshes over his shoes and some kind of shiny scarf around his neck. Sara's shoulders were bare that time, her hair was down. They stood for a long time talking in the entrance hall while a cloud of perfume and smoke floated up around the boys. Mark pretended to gag, Peter giggled and they were marched down to say hello. Mark saw how white Sara's shoulders were, as white and smooth as the white stone of a beautiful statue set high on a cliff above the ocean for sailors to see. Watching those shoulders, moving toward Sara, Mark had decided that he did not like the man with her, not at all. Everything about the man was small and quick, from his little glittery eyes to the triangular beard on the tip of his chin, to the way he bowed when they said their pleased-to-meet-yous.

That's all he'd known about Sara until one Saturday just past when he'd come bumping down the stairs and found Sara standing in the entrance hall with his mother. "Remember what we talked about last week?" his mother had asked. "Well, this is Sara who will teach you to swim."

"Hello, Sara who will teach me to swim," he'd mumbled. And here they are.

"Well, what would you say is your biggest problem with swimming? What I'm asking is how do you see it, Mark?" Her voice is low, rich, and clear. It has a sound he can't quite place but it's soothing as if something like Grandmother's peach brandy with lemon was in it. What he sees is only right in front of him, all around him: *water*, can she help?

"I get scared when I get to the deep end," he says, "and then I choke." That's what the other teachers said when they gave up and handed him back to his parents – can't do a thing with him, he chokes. With both hands he grabs himself around the neck, says *aargh* and falls backwards into the water to show her what he means. She hauls him up. Is her face friendly? It is; in fact, she's *laughing*. He smiles up at that face which is surrounded by a lot of coppery hair. Her hand comes up, a stumpy hand with bitten-back nails and harsh knuckles as if she'd been out in the cold a lot without gloves or had her hands in water every day. He relaxes a little under that hand's weight.

Around the pool, two girls from his seventh-grade class giggle when Sara touches his shoulder, takes his hand. At the other end of the pool, tall windows rinse and weep with steam, the colors of the sunset run down them. Sara makes him walk deeper, chest-deep, anchored to her hand. It's awful to be held, to need to be held, to turn to her and cling like a monkey. His heart pounds so hard it thuds down in his knees. Awful. He knows his ribs are showing, just like a scrawny dog's, giving him away, and he wishes he weren't so thin that *everything* showed. He doesn't belong here, he belongs back in that body, boneless as a puppy's, padded with flesh to hide it, that now belongs to Peter. Yes, that's it: that body wriggles, goes limp, falls down, and people come running.

"Good enough," she says, she has a quick nervous smile. "Could you swim out and turn around and swim back, just so I can get an idea of what your problem is?"

"Swim out?" he echoes. "Sure." She lets go of his hand, he feels the current stop. Then he's off, one arm cocked to stroke. Right away, as he knew it would, water rushes up his nose and trickles down the back of his throat. He squeezes his eyes shut and, blinded, he rolls his head and grabs a breath, kicks, plunges and drives his arms into the water.

Then the water seems to thicken, he's tangled in it, and the fear shoots out through his arms and legs, making them weak. He hears his breath rasp in his ears but it's only a *sound* because no *air* comes in and what does come in gets blocked by a hard place high up in his chest, and disappears, leaving him nothing. And so at last, with his eyes squeezed tight, he lifts his head again to steal a breath and in his hurry breathes water and stands up choking, water streaming from his mouth and nose. As he gags, he reaches for something, finds SARA right there, lifting him up as though she's been there by his side all along.

Sara is a tall woman. His mother is tall too, and a woman, but she's soft, without Sara's angles. So Sara is not his mother. There are other reasons, all of them confusing, why Sara is not his mother. Sara has muscles in her arms and legs, long flat swimmer's muscles that stand up in her arms when she grabs him and saves him from choking or sinking, when she supports him with her arms so he can practice his stroke. Sara's legs are slender and white and dusted with reddish-brown hair, soft as feathers. His mother's calves are round and white, they mush together when she crosses her legs and *her* arms are also white and soft, like the white fragrant skin on her face and neck.

Also, there is the way Sara looks in the water. He cannot imagine his mother in the water except as he's always seen her — sunk into a silver plastic float, greased and wearing sunglasses. But Sara, Sara *grew* in water. He doesn't think about Sara; at least he doesn't *try* to think about Sara but sometimes he'll be walking along, scuffing the sidewalk and thinking of nothing when he realizes that he has stopped and is staring up through the pale green and flickering light that young leaves make around a tree, and he'll see Sara standing in the pool, see the scar on her thigh, a thick twisting white line with stitch-marks down either side that disappears into the water just below where her legs come together. He cannot look at that spot where her legs meet without thinking of the statues, women all bare and white, nothing held back, with breasts of stone that look soft enough to touch, with long curved bellies leading you down, only right where their legs meet the statues are broken, right where you want to see they've been broken off and set on marble pedestals, or water.

The lilac bush near the porch steps begins to sprout new buds all along its downy branches and he waits outside for Sara every night. He crouches behind the lilac bush with his bathing suit and towel across his knees, fitting himself into the roots where they stand up above the ground. That way he can see her before she sees him. Some nights are pale as milk and shrouded, the streetlights flare behind the fog and the night is full of the thin splashing sounds of water dripping from the trees. Other nights are bright, tense with stars, some so bright they are magnets, pulling other stars toward their brightness.

On the thick nights he's thoughtful, quiet, wrapped in the fog and drifting, the way he used to feel when they bundled him out of the car half-asleep and carried him up to bed. On the tense nights the pull of the stars makes an ache in his chest, as though something of the stars' magnetism were there, a compressed energy pulling everything toward its center. His eyes feel sharp, exploding against the light, golden as any animal's. Those nights he jumps and claps and dances crazily all over the lawn.

He loves to watch Sara swim. She makes it look easy, she makes it a promise. She shoves off straight as a blade, parting the water, then her arm comes up like the wing of a swan, then down and up again, trailing water like feathers. Sara insists it's only a matter of patience and practice. But he knows better — it's something she knows, something she can give him. "Look," she says, "I cannot do it for you. I had to learn just like you."

"You did not," he says, "Sara, you never had to learn."

"Oh go on."

But he knows the truth: it's magic, she's got the secret, she gives it. And if this isn't true then why — when she lifts his arms for him or turns his head and makes him breathe — does he understand, and why — when she lets go — does he falter and sink? One night everything works and he shoots through the water, arms and legs graceful, supple as sea grass, and then he's scared of the power running up his arms and legs and he chokes and stops. But those few seconds are like another time not long before, when the choir at school had practiced and practiced the chorus of "The Battle Hymn of the Republic," trying to get it right. They'd adjusted, readjusted, bass voices holding, sopranos ringing clear, then they'd hit upon it all at once: a shared constellation of notes, the center of the notes itself a note that nobody sang but everybody heard all around them so that they were no longer outside, they were inside something larger. And when they were quiet again, it seemed that the sound still hung in the air, rippling out like the sound a bell leaves after it has stopped ringing. So *that*, he thinks, rising out of the water triumphant, is how it feels to swim — it feels like singing when all the voices sound right.

For weeks, this goes on and on. Sara coaxes, cajoles, Sara has a thousand faces. One day she pretends to tear her hair and he recoils, pretending to fear. The next day she coaxes him, chucks him under the chin, holds him up, turns his head, lifts his arms to show him how it's done, while he giggles and holds his breath, feeling her breasts so close they nearly brush the back of his neck. Sara is the one who drives the panic from him. All he need do is stand up choking and she's right there, thumping him on the back, wiping the water out of his eyes tenderly, tenderly. This goes on and on. One night the lines in her face — she has a fine cross-hatching near the eyes, a few deep grooves around her mouth — all pull down, and she says: "Look here, son, you are a most especially difficult person."

"It's no use, Sara," he says, paddling at the water, "I know I'll be the same as soon as you're gone."

"That's crap," she says. "And you're just going to have to grow up."

"Yes, Sara," he answers, "you're the boss." But when her anger passes she looks tired and he's sorry because he meant it only as a game for *both* of them to play, a game like cowboys, where you get tied up so tight the helplessness feels delicious.

One night, not many nights later, he sees that the overlapping petals of the crocuses beside the walk have unclenched to reveal rough golden tongues at their centers. He swoops without breaking stride and picks one and hands it to Sara as he slides into the car. "My mother told me to give you one of these," he says.

"Oh, well, tell her thank you then." Her voice, something's wrong. She touches the petals in a remote way and her eyes look swollen. She's wrapped in some kind of fuzzy shawl, the color of peaches, that comes all the way up to her chin, but despite the shawl she looks cold. She looks all alone across the seat of the car and he knows, he knows as surely as if he smelled it – that a man caused this, the one with the cigarette and galoshes. On the way to the pool, his fists open and close at his sides. He wants to protect her, he feels her distance. That night, though she holds him as always, something is missing. No strength flows from her hands as she moves his arms and counts for him. He feels small without that strength. When he looks up, she's staring off through the wall of glass at the far end of the pool. That night, the water feels chilly, and he makes himself helpless in order to bring her back, but she lets him go. He floats right off her hands away from her and he wants to strike out at her to end his helplessness and bring her back but he

44

cannot reach her. How can she be so far away when her body is so close, touching his, holding him up?

"Sara, watch," he says, rolling off her hands. "Sara, look, I'm a porpoise. Now, Sara, look, I'm a jack-in-the-box. Now, Sara, too bad, I've drowned."

"Hooray," Sara says after each trick, and she claps her hands without making a sound.

At home that night it seems he has walked into a houseful of strangers in strange rooms. His father and mother are sitting on the couch in front of the TV, with Peter sprawled across her lap. Blue TV shadows wash over them, and laughter. He is in no mood for laughter. He tiptoes out the way he came, pats the pockets of his father's jacket which hangs on the back of a kitchen chair, finds a cigarette and runs away down the sidewalk and into the grove of trees in the vacant lot at the end of the street. This is the place — a wood lot on the edge of a field, with its steep-sided drainage ditch, its grove of sycamore saplings standing white and straight as rays of light among the darker oaks and hickories — that is battlefield, playground, and home in the wilderness for boys from up and down the street. He walks into the grove until he comes to the sycamore where he carved his initials five years before, reaches up and touches the letters where they have been carried until they are almost as high as the lowest branches. Soon, he thinks, they will be so high only the stars will see them. He sits with his back against this tree and looks out across the field which is turned up now, turbulent with steep black humps of earth.

He sits there hugging his knees and bows his head on the

top of his arms and says *Sara*, hoping to trap her name in the hollow of his body and to let the sound of it help him with this feeling that comes over him when he thinks of her – a steady glowing in his chest so bright at the center that it tugs at the rest of him, pulling him toward that bright core. He lights his cigarette and inhales, feeling the same moody pleasure he sees on his father's face when he smokes. The cigarettes are something new, something he does now and again, and when he smokes he can *see* his face reflected back to him the way it will look someday when the coarse black hair, the slumbering eyes, gray with flecks of gold, have made him handsome.

As he sits there, remembering his face, smoking and thinking of Sara, it occurs to him who Sara looks like. Of course, the way her hair swoops down over her forehead, the way her eyes get round and sad sometimes, she looks like the famous actress he saw last month on TV, the one in the movie that was full of heavy sorrowful speeches and carriages rolling along snowy streets, the one with the famous scene which made his mother and father say "Ah" together. This scene happened in an old-fashioned time in an old-fashioned room full of heavy chairs, with crystals dangling from the vases and lamps. A soldier in his uniform stood over the famous woman who was dressed in black and sat in a chair, working at some sewing. The man wore ribbons on the pockets of his uniform, ropes of gold braid hung from each shoulder. He said he was leaving for the war and he'd swelled a little when he said that. He had an impatient and feverish look. He kept talking, he said blah blah blah and then she looked up – her eyes had been sad all her life – and she said *"What war?"* with such quiet hatred and bewilderment that the man's face, all his braid, everything about him stopped and that's when his mother and father said "Ah" together. His mother wiped her eyes, his father slapped both knees and stood up the way he did when something was decided. "Well," he said, "looks like she showed him the door," which was confusing since not long after that scene, the woman went out and walked through the snow at night and threw herself in front of a train.

Afterwards, when he asked why they'd said "Ah" like that together, his mother said it was because that scene was the moment in the film when you recognized their tragedy, that's when you saw how far apart the man and the woman were from each other, and the woman had already given up everything for him. Mark was content with that answer at the time because it didn't matter, it was just a dumb movie, but now, reviewing it in his mind, seeing it again before his eyes, it seems real in a funny way, and it matters. It matters because when Sara becomes that famous woman sitting in her chair and the man stands over her looking lost, he sees what his mother meant by how far apart they were. She meant that look on their faces, which was how two creatures from different universes would look if they ran into each other in the dark. She meant the things they said: *war*, he said, and she said *what?* and their words fell heavy and wet as late spring snow, sticking to everything, melting within the hour. She meant the way *he* feels when Sara says *swim* and he stands there in the water wondering *how?*

Wait a minute. Silence comes down around him as though a big door had swung shut, closing him in a silent room the size of the universe. Out on the harrowed field, shreds of fog drift and hover over the low spots. In the distance Prairie du Chien glitters, a mass of lights. Wait a minute. If he doesn't know what she means when she says *swim* then he is like the man, the soldier. He stands up, agitated. *No*, something shouts in his mind. He peels off big slabs of new green bark from the sycamore. *Yes*, something else shouts back and he sees himself growing, he is turning into a *man* – black hair, gray eyes, cigarette, all of him growing through the stages like evolution done in time lapse – lumbering ape to gape-mouthed hairy creature to man, standing upright, everything shrunk and smoothed into the right proportions. And where is Sara? With the others, standing over there, different, in another world that did not come about in the same way, her world, not his. The thought of it makes him so agitated that he stubs the cigarette out against the tree and runs for home. Home to where his mother is just closing the refrigerator door when he comes in, a glass of milk in one hand and her face all creamed and shining for the night. "I heard you coming," she says, and hands him the milk.

Some children make marks on doorjambs to measure how they grow. He keeps a list taped to the nightstand beside his bed, written on the back of an old adding-machine tape so it can get as long as it needs to, of the strokes and kicks he's working to learn: flutter kick, frog kick, breast- and side-strokes, Australian crawl (sort of), how to tread water, how to read Sara's face, how to make Sara pluck him out of the water. Flounder, choke, pretend to drown, look blank. If there were time, the list would go on forever because he would go on forever trying to get close to her.

He wakes up one morning troubled and angry. The light is soft across the back yard and his brother Peter sleeps with open mouth mashed against the pillow and something is wrong, wrong, wrong. His body feels sour and tired, as though he's dreamt of fighting and can't remember how it went or who won. On the bureau across the room, the goldfish hangs in its bowl, tail stirring the water. The closet door is shut and locked so no ghosts can get Peter in the night, and on the wall calendar two fighter planes spiral down out of black clouds edged with fire. That's what's wrong, the calendar is what's wrong. Today is April twentieth. May fifteenth is marked – end of swimming with Sara – and the gap between the two, which once seemed so wide it could never be crossed, is narrow now, and closing.

That night at the pool his stroke falls to pieces. He kicks and holds his breath until he turns red, churns with his arms and kicks spasmodically, chokes, and his arms and legs lock in fear. He clings to Sara when she pulls him out. She says "What is wrong with you?" as she tries to look into his eyes. "All of a sudden you go deaf, dumb, and blind. You forget everything we've learned. It all begins with breathing, remember? You just breathe from *here*." She touches him, lays her *palm* on the center of his chest, right on the breastbone, and he gets very still, his whole *body* listens as all the light and all the warmth slowly slowly rise and gather under that spot where she's put her hand. While she watches with her look – like she's laughing so much inside it's filled up her eyes.

"Yes Sara," he can hardly speak. "You're the boss."

"Oh grow up," she says. The hand is gone, she's taken it back.

49

He grows up. "Sara, seriously now, I want to swim just like you. I don't want to quit until I can swim just like you."

She purses her lips, lays a finger there. "Well look," she says, "it's time for you to think about the facts of life here, my dear. I'm leaving in two weeks." She holds up two fingers to make her point. "So if you're going to do any learning you'd better do it fast."

Sara? Leaving? "Where are you going?" he says, thinking of the man, the soldier, thinking of himself and of the lights of Prairie du Chien far away across the tumbling field.

"Vacation," she shrugs, then seeing his eyes she says, "Well now I'll be back. If you forget something we can have a refresher lesson. Or somebody else could take up where I leave off. Look, you can't expect to have me around forever now can you?"

"So where are you going?" he asks, making his voice bold and casual, too, the way he's heard it done.

"Europe," she says, "with a friend. We're going to bicycle around France and Spain."

"What friend?" he asks, then jumps to answer himself, "*I* know, the one who makes you cry."

Her face does a dance, smiles, frowns, her face stops cold. "You don't know a thing, my love," she says, tapping him on the nose.

Well, he knows that's true and he flings himself away and swims underwater as fast as possible till he thinks his lungs will crack. He's a prisoner escaping, the only way out is through a long tunnel filled with water. Rising, he slaps the water with the palms of both hands then ducks and she ducks, she's coming toward him underwater, hair waving all around her head, eyes bugging out. He comes up gasping, clings to her.

"Don't go," he says. "I haven't learned to swim yet, Sara, but I'll go swimming anyway and I'll drown, then how'll you feel?" Her head hangs to one side, mouth open, and he thinks *she doesn't know what to say*, and he glows a little. Sara the talker, the quick one, is mute. He's won.

Then the last day of swimming lessons is upon him. He's counted, re-counted the days, hoping each time to discover a mistake, a few days misplaced, or more fingers, a new way to count. Mornings, his parents must tear the sheets back and command him to get up. On those mornings, they talk above and around him as if he weren't there, the sort of talk that infuriates him. It goes like this – munching his toast, his father says that it's a great mystery to him why, if the boy's in such a hurry to get to that pool with Sara, he doesn't want to get up in the mornings. "Do you understand that, Mama?" he asks, and Mark closes his eyes against the lie of her answer, the mild surprise in her voice. "No, I must confess," she says, "I'm baffled by it, completely baffled."

In the water that night, he practices as long as he's able, and the clock, for once, cooperates. Still, they come to it too soon. The pool's almost empty, people hoist themselves out and dawdle away. They disappear, dripping, into the dressing rooms. Then it's time.

"Well kid, it's time," Sara says. "Are you ready?" He wishes she wouldn't call him "kid." He wishes he could say no.

Instead, he gives the speech he has prepared: "It's very dangerous where I'm going, Sara," he says. "Maybe you had better come along too just to make sure I'm all right."

She brushes hair out of his eyes, her hand rests on his shoulder: "You'd better get going then, hadn't you?" For once, she's not trying to keep from laughing. "If I come with you then you haven't learned to swim, have you?" He shakes his head *no*, no answer to give to that question except to go where she's telling him he has to go, where he never wanted to go in the first place, except to please her.

On tiptoes he approaches the red stripe that separates the shallow from the deep water and stares down the long gradual slope out to where the blue water turns deeper and bluer blue. Another question begins to form and he looks back to ask it. "Sara," he begins, "what if?"

"Swim," she says. And he throws himself over the line, thrashing at the water as though he were fighting, striking out at anything that moves. Meanwhile, the familiar clutching begins in his chest, something is squeezing his lungs, making them so small no air can get in. He tries to picture Sara holding him up, but she's not there, only the water is there, Sara is behind him now. She's gone. He lifts his head and looks at the end of the pool and up into the wall of dark glass at the end of the pool, sees the pool stretching backwards and himself, a blur in the water and Sara behind him, almost out of sight. He starts to flounder, feels himself sinking. Float, Sara said, if you feel yourself starting to panic then float, so he floats — arms out, eyes closed, not looking down. *Don't think about how deep the water is*. That's what she said. Don't think about where you're going, just think about swimming, just breathe, kick, pull, breathe, kick, pull. So he gathers himself and begins to kick and work his arms until he levels out in the water, begins to stroke and roll his head and breathe and he feels it, it's

happening, it works – he's swimming, he's *swimming*. The
water moves out of his way and he is master of the water
for once, he could go on forever. I'm swimming, he thinks,
Sara, I'm swimming away from you. Then he bumps the
wall of the pool and clings there gasping and smiling at
nothing. From far away, back at the other end, Sara calls.
"Hey," she yells, "hey you there in the deep end." But for
now, he pretends not to hear.

There will come a time, years later, when a woman will
touch him and pull him under, back to this night, and it
will all come back to him – the panic first, the gulping,
gasping feel of panic, then jubilation, freedom, then something else that he had forgotten. They will be lying in a
room in his basement apartment with the window open
and the rain steady on the earth and a thick blue stub of
candle burning beside the mattress, the kind of light he likes
for lovemaking, for the way it quickens and subsides, for
the mystery it makes of faces and bodies.

As she moves under him and he moves with her, he will
feel panic begin to rise, shutting off his air, and spread out
through his body until he feels himself disappearing, unable
to move, unable to breathe or pull. He will struggle up to
try and see her face, to find himself again, but she will pull
him down, the candle flame will rock shadows all over the
room. She will pull until he lets go as he's learned to do, to
the rocking that he recognizes now as the rocking of trees
against the starlight, the tight look of buds along limbs, the
lost star at the center of himself around which everything
tightened, and all, every one, is desire and he gives himself
over to it. Until she opens out in front of him, opens, then

closes again and he opens like a gill, a hungry mouth, and just at the moment when he feels himself so deep inside her he is nothing but this rocking and swaying, he feels a shift, a stir, and though she holds him there, wants and keeps him there, he feels himself pushed out, rocked free, wave after wave carrying him out, away.

They will lie apart then, touching, and when he feels lonely again for that place where he lost himself, he will haul himself back on top of her and watch her face. He will lift the fine strands of hair that are stuck to her forehead, one by one. He will touch and hold each breast while she strokes him up and down his back, smiling up at him and watching through those Egyptian-dark eyes, and he will start to talk. He will try and tell her everything, everything he knows about how it feels to be taken in and then set free. He will clench and unclench his fist to show her what he means when he talks about entering and leaving this world where men come and go. He will talk about how you leave only to enter again and always into the same world so that no leaving is ever final or free. And then his voice will slow, and then it will stop because she has held a hand over his mouth, a soft hand, sharp with salt. She will press her hips up against him, say "Sssh, don't talk," and he will enter her and feel himself drawn back toward that place again before he can say what he wants to say, what he never gets to say, before he can tell somebody that the world where women live has no end, it is round, it has only beginnings and everything comes back to the place where it began.

He will groan then, and press his face into the warm hollow of her shoulder and neck, and see himself again in the pool that night a long time ago, paddling back toward Sara and feeling that longing, that loneliness for his old floundering, helpless self, the one lifted out again and again, the one held close. And he will hold to her then and press his face deeper into her neck, under her hair, and with his eyes shut tight, he will see his shadow beneath him on the floor of the pool and remember how cold it looked, cold and far away.

This is how he goes toward that night. As she promised way back in the beginning, Sara takes him hiking, a reward for learning to swim. Saturday, he's up before dawn, dressed, waiting. When he hears her car door slam, hair prickles along the back of his neck and his heart jumps around inside his rib cage. He flings on his day pack and runs down the stairs in time to see his father press a check into Sara's hand. His mother stands there beaming, her eyes lit up and moist as if it were Christmas morning. Well, of course they *paid* her. She didn't do it for her *health*, stupid, she didn't do it for herself. She did it for him, for them. He feels like a stick figure of a little man as he stands there shouldering his pack. And Sara too has changed. She's heavier through the hips, her clothes are plain – jeans and a shirt buttoned up around her neck, an old green sweater with a raveled spot sewn up with red thread. "Chilly for May," she says, rubbing her hands, which are chapped, as usual. Her eyelashes and lips look almost colorless and she has that dopey wide-eyed stare of people who wear contact lenses.

"Where are we going?" he asks, studying the toe of his shoe. When she names the state park not five miles away, he sighs and humps the pack higher on his back.

They park the car in the gravel lot and take a trail that leads away from a manmade lake where a few power boats mutter and hum. They find themselves climbing up a worn, narrow trail lined with hickory and maple trees. His father says maples are junk trees, Mark tells her. He skips to catch up with her, to tell about the man who chain-sawed one out of their front yard. She wheels to face him: "There's no such thing as junk in nature," she says. He drops back, stung. He's not his father so why does she rebuke him? Her hair is plaited in one long pigtail, thin as a China-man's. His chest feels tight. There's a sleepy trickling of thought, a flow through his mind, and it goes like this: *where are we going, Sara*, spoken in time with their steps.

They walk till they come to a wide grassy patch at the top of a hill and they sit down there to eat. He unpacks their lunch, bowing each time as he presents her with sandwich or pickle. He loads her down with food and they sit chewing in silence until he says: "Sara, where did you grow up?"

"A place called Mobile, Alabama," she says. He's never known anyone from the South.

"Is it exciting there?"

"It's really flat," she says, "and God it's hot. But there are boats, too. Mobile is the only part of Alabama that touches the Gulf of Mexico and there are the most wonderful sea birds. I'd never go back there though, I sure wouldn't." Her face looks darker, and sad, as though a sliding screen covered with dark paper has moved across it.

"Do they have boys like me there?" he asks, and holds himself still, listening for the *no* he can almost *hear* her say. *No, there's no one just like you.*

56

Her mouth stops chewing: "You're a funny person." Her eyes look beyond him. "I expect they have boys like you almost everywhere."

"Oh," he says glumly, and he's falling, fading into the crowd of all the boys in the world. He's disappearing, folded up, a small thing, like that bird he and Peter found one spring, dead and folded up inside its broken blue egg shell. He remembers how the jackknifed legs, the sharp fan of wing bones covered with a thin membrane of transparent skin, the small hard beak, had been folded, tucked and bent until the bird was as round as the shell. He feels the same fear begin as he'd felt that day when he'd dropped the shell to break it completely and watched the bird come open on the ground, and he gropes for a way out. He thinks of the soldier in the room with the famous woman, the way he shimmers in his braid, the way he carries himself so tall and straight. He leans over and touches Sara's leg where he knows the white scar will be below the denim cloth. She stops chewing and watches him, her eyes serious and mocking him at the same time. But he plunges on. "Sara," he says, "I've been wondering the whole time I've known you where you got that scar." Her mouth keeps smiling but her eyes darken and watch, taking in everything.

"Well, goodness, you could have asked any time," she says, her voice is brisk, like his mother's voice when he asks her certain things. "When I was about ten I was running and not looking where I was going and I ran into a tree and cut my leg. Stupid, huh?" She stands up, leaving the half-eaten bread on the ground. *Sara, where are you going?* It's the clothes. Something's wrong. He touched her all the time at the pool. And she touched him. He touched her there

but he can't touch her here and the pool was only two days
before and things are all mixed up. It's wrong: Sara's eyes
are troubled; there's turbulence all around her, a disturbance
of the air. It terrifies and excites him and mingles with the
pulse that began when he touched her and beats all around
him like a giant heart and he wants to touch her again
and knows he must not. This way lies power, he feels it.
He is strong, drawing strength from her confusion. She's
looking around, distracted, perhaps lost. He'll protect her;
he'll smooth back her hair and lay her out beside the fire.
They'll curl together to keep from freezing. It will be his
world and she will stay there waiting for the news he brings,
for the food.

"Are we lost?" he says.

"Of course not," she says. "How could we be lost when
everything is marked as plain as day." She shows him a
blue arrow slashed into a tree that points to a path that
leads into the woods, a path so wide and smooth a blind
person could follow it. She takes a deep breath. "Coming?"
she asks. He has to gather up the things and run after her
and he catches up with her where the trail leaves the woods
and runs along the top of the railroad cut. She walks fast,
swinging her arms, and he follows her, looking down into
the deep dry gulch to where the tracks run along the bottom.
"Sara," he says, "wait." Just as they reach the point where
the trail turns back into the woods a whistle sounds from
down the track, then another, closer this time, a shrill blast,
close as an alarm.

"Listen," he claps, "there's a train. Let's stay and watch
it, please, Sara. I really like trains you know, I always have,"
he says, trying to reach her with his voice. The agitation

has gone from around her, she's just Sara again, friendly and sturdy as a wall.

"Just for a minute," she says. "I need to go home soon." *Sara, where are you going?*

She sits down at a distance from him, hands clasped around her drawn-up knees. He smells hot metal, iron. At home, from his bed late at night, he can hear trains whistling, clanking and grappling. The sounds are something the wind brings in through the window. Now the sound is all around them, rolling, like a million drums, and the smell of the tracks is the smell of the air. Sara is speaking through the noise that fills his head. "Excuse me?" he says.

"I said, I bet you wanted to be an engineer when you were little," she shouts.

"*No,*" he shouts back, hoping that the noise of the passing train will hide the bitterness. How can she be so ordinary?

The cars flash by: bright, dull, bright again while the noise blasts higher into the air until it seems the air is made of noise; the trees shimmer behind light and noise. Empty boxcars, cars filled with shiny lumps of coal, a car full of cattle, rolling eyes pressed to the slatted sides, an empty flatbed car with a jammed wheel that screams against the track, a car with a white heart painted on the side – *Heart of Dixie* written in script inside the heart. "Sara, look quick," he screams, "look, that's where you're from." She frowns into the sun, makes the O.K. sign, a circle with thumb and forefinger, and his own heart rests again. The tall leaning shadows of the cars slip over them. There are white cars with bright orange arrows and yellow stripes, older cars, bright cars, then the caboose comes rocking into view.

He stands up to go. Sara stands up too. He's half turned away when he sees the man in the little bay window of the caboose. Mark can't tell if the man is young or old. He's dressed in gray — gray shirt, gray trousers, pale hair that could be either gray or blond. The man is staring, out of the window, at the walls of the gulch, he is touching himself lightly with one hand. When he looks up and sees them standing there he takes his hand away and his face breaks into a child's wide smile. He raises a gloved hand and waves, a big broad wave as if he's waving a lantern, and then the caboose is gone, wagging off down the track with the sound following it away. Mark stands very still. He *knows* that man, and that man is going somewhere. He wants to run after him and find out, to run and run straight down that track until he catches up with the train and makes the man tell where he's going. "Hey," he yells into the gulch, "hey, hey." His fists are clenched, he feels his face getting hot. While Sara waits to take him home.

In Darkness

~~~~~ THE SUMMER Jennifer was ten, her grandfather Turner said she must learn to be silent with the rest of them. It had been a time of abrupt decisions – loud voices, suitcases packed in the middle of the night, lights snapped on, cars that scraped the low spot at the end of the driveway, tires that squealed all the way back into the garage – and she'd discovered that the way to get along was to make herself small and to follow wherever they led. In May, her mother and father had decided that this year she would spend two months in Hamilton with Grandma and Grandpa Turner because Mommy was going away for a while and summer was Daddy's busy season at Kodak. "Besides," they'd asked, crouched in front of her grinning and looking excited the way they did when they wanted to make something sound like fun, "wouldn't it be great to be in Hamilton for that long?" She'd studied them, and then she'd said yes, because she understood that *yes* was the only answer they'd hear. And when her grandmother said she must choose one dress to wear to meeting on Sundays, she chose a plain blue dress with a round collar and red smocking at the waist and wrists. And when her grandfather said she must learn to be still with the other Quakers, she left behind the colored pencils and paper that had distracted her through other

summer meetings, and she sat with her hands folded like the rest of them, waiting, watching the sunlight slowly take the room, one wall at a time, dissolving the white boards in light.

The meeting house was a gaunt one-room building with gray benches and plain tall windows. The people (like their house, she thought) were also plain and clean. Sitting among them that summer, Jennifer counted colors in the room – her red smocking, green shutters, red stovepipe on the wood stove – and secretly felt proud to find herself among them. The women wore dark dresses, muted patterns; the men smelled of smoke, they wore white shirts, gray pants. After the greetings, the shifting, and coughing had subsided, they were quiet together. At first, there was just the ordinary comfortable quiet of people sitting together in a room. But then the silence stirred and came to life. Every Sunday she listened and watched for the moment of the change, but she always missed it. From the bare polished floor to the sharply pitched roof the silence moved among them and deepened, the way light fills a room through a clear window. It was as if the silence had always been there and the people came into it one by one until no one was left outside. And when the people were listening together inside the silence, their faces changed – they softened and rested as if the silence had stopped in front of each person and quieted each face. No longer fierce, sad, hungry – the way her mother had looked before she left for Pittsburgh – they looked like people who'd found something they'd lost, something they recognized. Her grandfather said they were resting from toil. For Jennifer, there always came a moment when the room was so deep in stillness, the light so clear, they might all have been floating in an ocean of silence and light. Each time, just at this moment, a shiver danced straight up her back and she wished she could stay there. She shut her eyes then and tried to hold onto the feeling but it faded in front of her and was gone by the time someone said "Amen."

At home, in her grandparents' house, she often checked her own face, expecting to find a change. She stared into the dark, bright eyes, and sometimes, just as she turned away from the mirror, she thought she caught a glimpse of another expression similar to the one on the people's faces when the silence was deepest.

Every Sunday as they drove home, she'd ask: "What were the people looking for?" And every Sunday, Grandpa Turner prompted her, his eye with its wild, white eyebrow fixed on her in the rearview mirror: "What do we say?"

"Light," she'd say, bored with the answer. The leaves of the young willows that lined the streambed beside the road flashed silver when a breeze stirred them, and she wondered if that was the light they meant, the underside of what you could see.

"That's correct," he'd always say. "We call it light."

"But where does it come from? What's it for?"

Sometimes her grandfather would only say that the light was invisible, and this light was what made us live.

"How can you see it then?"

"With other eyes," he'd say. She giggled at the thought. He looked stern as a mountain when he talked that way. He said the people were looking for the light inside them and the only way to find the light was to be very still, to go into the dark and look.

"The dark?"

"What you see when you close your eyes," he said. "That's what we are, and the light is inside the dark."

Her Grandmother Turner would get impatient then and say, "It's what we have in common, Jennifer. It's what we all have been given and what we want and give to each other." But no one could describe this light or say it starts here, ends there, this is its shape; and if we all had it in common, then why did we have to work so hard to find it, why did we have to be so still?

"Because," her grandfather said, "that's how we're made. This is the light that banishes the inner dark," he said.

"What's *banish*?" It sounded black and cold and far away.

"Sent away," he said. She understood then. Love did it. And love was what you waited for too. "Just you wait," they'd say. "Just wait till your mother comes home, what a good time you'll all have again."

So she waited. She couldn't remember a slower summer. The days in Hamilton passed as heavily as the man who came in June to set the beehives in her grandfather's orchard. Dressed in padded gray clothes and gloves, with a net over his face, the man moved among the apple trees in his clumsy dance. Always before, she had raced him, keeping to the edges of the orchard, taking pleasure in her bare legs and the speed with which she'd outrun him. That summer, she sat and watched him from the top of a small grassy hill nearby, feeling as swaddled and hindered as the man in his quilted garments. Even the bees seemed sluggish that summer. Some years, they worked fast, speeding from blossom to blossom, their legs furred with pollen. Some years, they

66

buried themselves so deeply in the blossoms they might have been parts of flowers. But that year it was cold and damp until late June, and the bees, if they left the hives at all, flew clumsily from tree to tree and dropped heavily into the flowers. It wasn't even fun to run after them, they were so easy to follow. That was the summer she found out about waiting. The Quakers waited too, but they got what they wanted. She waited, but the trouble was she didn't know what she was waiting for, only that it would be different once it came. It seemed she'd have to wait even to know what she was waiting for.

Late in July her father took her back to Webster's Crossroads. Her mother arrived August eleventh on the 2:05 bus from Pittsburgh, and her father took a vacation so he could be with her. They talked from the time they left the bus station in Rochester until they passed the last suburb and dropped into the valley where Webster's Crossroads lay. The closer they got to home, the less her mother talked and the more she stared out the window. Finally, even her father was quiet. At home, he'd taped balloons to all the door frames and they'd lettered a paper banner that read *Welcome Home*. Her mother blushed and smiled and fingered the edge of the banner and then she set her suitcase in the front hall just inside the door. When Jennifer and her father grabbed the handle she said, "Just leave it there, please, I'll get it later."

"Not on your life," he said.

Mommy got very patient then. She pressed her lips together: "Just leave it there, I said." But he picked up the suitcase anyway and he said: "Margaret, it's all right, just relax." Her mother walked heavily upstairs then and took a shower and had a drink and Jennifer understood, with a sinking feeling, that whatever was supposed to have begun when Mommy came home had already begun and ended.

Later, after dark, her mother gathered Jennifer up into her lap and tried to tell her their story about the great tree that grows between heaven and earth and about how the stars over the valley behind the house are really the buds and leaves of this tree. But she forgot one part of the story, mixed up another, and Jennifer grew more and more restless until finally she interrupted: "Mother," she said, "you know Pegasus? Well, he's just stars in the *shape* of a horse." Her mother sat very still, blinking hard, and then she leaned over and kissed Jennifer on the top of her head and said, "Right you are, honey," and she went inside. That was her mother's first day at home.

The second day was no better, nor the third. They visited every boring place they'd ever been. They visited the two wineries nearby, and as usual her parents sipped wine and allowed her one small sip. They visited every musty antique store along the highway. She knew the contents of these stores so well she could have walked through the rooms blindfolded, naming the things no one ever bought: stuffed rooster, butter churn, dented milk pail, photograph made on tin. That was boring enough, but Coneseus Lake was the last straw. She and her father had been there to swim almost every day since she'd come home. Now she had to be ordered out of the car and lifted into the rowboat, the *Hughes III*, named after the three of them. She would have been content to wait on shore, to look up and find the boat, shading her eyes against the glare, and then to go on building her own pathways and walls out of the freckled pebbles that felt smooth and cool as the lake itself when she stroked them with her thumb.

But no. Her mother snapped, her father scowled. They hustled her into the rowboat and her father said she was part of this family too, and she might as well get used to it. He rowed them into the center of the lake where the water was deep and, even in August, cold. And he made them bow their heads and hold hands and swear: "Till death do us part, again," he said. And when he said *death* she thought *the lake*, he means the lake, and she felt a chill, as if the sun had set without warning and the night cold had seeped through the bottom of the boat and was swirling around their ankles like fog. He squeezed her hand and she squeezed her mother's hand but neither of them opened their eyes. She looked around and saw that they were alone on the lake, the sun was sinking, and the shore seemed far away and rapidly darkening. A loon flew overhead, trailing its clear mournful call. Daddy switched on the big square flashlight and set it on the seat up near the bow. Mother held out her hands to its beam, then laughed, tucked her hands back between her knees while Daddy, with a look like glory on his face, leaned over from his seat to hers and brushed back a strand of hair that had caught in her mouth. Then there was only the sound of the small waves lapping against the sides of the boat. The quiet, the dark water seemed to Jennifer as trackless as the silence in Quaker meeting had been. "Light," her grandfather said. "The light is hidden inside the dark." She closed her eyes then and looked for the light and she saw the lake, a dark circle drawn around them, and the boat floating there with the light in the bow. They had gathered the light, she thought, drawing it out of the dimming sky, up from under the water, like fishermen drawing up their nets, until the boat was full of light and they rode with their catch home across the water. As her father rowed them back to shore she felt very solemn and grown-up.

The cookout to celebrate her mother's homecoming was Sunday night. They were grilling hamburgers in the back yard. Her father tossed the long-handled spatula with one hand and caught it behind his back with the other. His wedding ring glinted on his hand. Her mother didn't know, but Jennifer knew, that he'd rummaged through the house looking for the ring, which he'd taken off when she'd left. That broad band of white skin left by the ring had been the first thing she'd noticed when she'd come home from her grandparents' house in Hamilton. They'd said their rings were a sign of the love that would always be inside them. Well, what did the missing ring mean? No, it wasn't that love was gone. "Love doesn't do that," he'd explained one night not long after Jennifer came home from Hamilton. She couldn't sleep, had called to him. The night sounds — wind, sleepy birds, a big hoot owl, loud radio music downstairs — had seemed amplified, confused. She'd tried to concentrate on one sound but another intruded, then another until the sounds merged with the shadows tossed around the room by the sycamore outside her window, and mixed with a memory of her mother in her long dress, wearing a lacy white shawl around her shoulders. Then the sounds and the shadows tangled in a gust of wind, swooped and lifted to reveal the glimpse she'd gotten, before they'd hurried her away, of the girl who'd drowned that summer over in Hamilton. They had lifted her from the water still tangled in the branches of the fallen underwater tree that had pulled her down. "DADDY," she'd yelled.

Later, after he'd soothed her with talk of her mother, he'd said, "Just because Mother is gone right now doesn't mean she's stopped loving us or that we don't care about her, Jennifer." He'd smelled of beer and sounded distant. "No, I care too much," he'd said. And he sounded angry then, as though he were arguing with someone, the way her mother had sounded when she'd said she loved herself too, and that's why she had to go away for a while. That night Jennifer had thought he wanted to hit everything, only he couldn't decide where to begin. Then he'd shaken himself. "I'm sorry," he'd said. "Daddy's sorry." He'd smoked his cigarette carefully and knocked the ash off into his palm and sat there rolling it lightly so it didn't break up. "I believe time will prove me right about this, Jennifer, I do. And you must believe too," he said. So believe was what you must do. Believe in what? "Love changes," he said, "but it doesn't go away."

All summer, she'd watched the band of lighter skin on his ring finger darken, but it never blended with the brown of his hand. There was something repulsive about the white skin, something dead or private-looking, a mark that people shouldn't see.

Well, when Mommy said she was coming home, he sang "I'm Getting Married in the Morning," he put back on his wedding ring, cleaned the house, mowed half the lawn, rushed to Sears and bought a porch swing that he hung on the back porch just off the kitchen. "She has always wanted one of these," he said. That had been on Thursday. His ring fit perfectly down over the blank place, but Mommy didn't care for the swing. The night of the cookout, she asked, "Why the swing, Ed? It's almost autumn."

"Got a porch, Margaret, got to have a porch swing." He fanned the charcoal till it glowed. "It's like two plus two," he said.

Jennifer went over and hugged his legs for making it simple again. She looked up at him where he swayed over her, and she felt so safe she shouted: "Two plus two equals FOUR."

"Not so loud," her mother said.

"Right you are," her father said. "There are porch swings, sweetheart, and true love, flags, blue skies, the tall corn of Iowa, fathers and daughters, mothers and fathers, summertime, wheat fields, Webster's Crossroads, New York, and snowdrifts," he said, "and apples, and even Buffalo, New York."

She yelled "Daddy, what's those," gripping his pant legs, standing on his shoes.

"*Are* those," her mother corrected her. "It's just a tide of silliness, Jennifer," she said, shooting her daughter her shy, darting, sideways look, "just a tide and a flood of silliness. He's capable of that sometimes too, no matter what he says." She looks happy, Jennifer thought. The tense lines around her mouth and the dark look around her eyes were gone. She winked at Jennifer.

"It's a new day, Maggie," her father said. Daddy's happy, she thought. She remembered about happiness. Happiness was something to believe in. Happiness was part of the story that would start again – only it would be better –

now that her mother was home. Happiness made the story go. Her father came from the South. They'd met in college and had fallen desperately in love. They'd been so happy. Now they lived in New York State where Jennifer was born and everybody loved her because she was so pretty and sweet and made everyone happy. Mommy and Daddy loved Jennifer with all their hearts. And happiness was also what Mommy wanted when she went away – "A chance," she'd said, "for some happiness of my own." Still, Jennifer wondered. How could love and happiness send Mommy away in June and bring her back in August? And how did love and happiness make them speak to each other in those voices that made her shoulders pull tight? How could you ever know about love and happiness if they kept changing that way, like the lake with a storm coming – first silver, then gray?

Her mother went into the kitchen. They listened to her knocking around and swearing to herself. "Mommy's pretending she's forgotten where things are," her father whispered loudly to Jennifer.

"Mommy's not pretending anything." Her puzzled voice preceded her to the door, a slender woman in jeans and a green tank top piped in bright rainbow colors. "Where have you hidden everything?" she said.

"Have I?" he said. "I thought I put it all back in the right places." He winked at Jennifer.

"Oh, you," her mother said, and she ducked back inside.

"Mommy went to Pittsburgh," Jennifer said, carefully, quietly, and her father's hand bore down on the top of her head.

"Yes she did," he said. "And now she's back and that's

73

what we need to think about, isn't it?" Jennifer nodded. *Gone*, they said, was simply a catch, a pause. When *gone* ended, things returned to normal, meaning to love and happiness, she guessed. They said *normal* with grateful voices. But now normal hadn't come back. She couldn't explain. It wasn't like going to her room anymore and finding it familiar; it wasn't like crawling into their bed and taking a nap between them. Since her mother had come home, something didn't fit.

"Found it," her mother said, holding out a wooden salad bowl. His eyes changed, a light seemed to pass over them and he grabbed one of Margaret's fingers and wiggled it. "Eureka," he said, and he held onto the tip of her finger. She almost stumbled, frowned at her feet, at the two of them in the swing, and sat down on the porch's bottom step.

Jennifer climbed down from the swing and went to her mother, who was sucking an ice cube, her knees drawn up close to her chest. She put her arms around her mother's neck and kissed the back of her head and rubbed her nose in her mother's hair. It smelled of milk and made her drowsy. She leaned, her mother turned, and Jennifer kissed the air. "Honey," her mother said, "honey, Mommy loves you but she doesn't want you leaning on her right now, all right? It's too warm."

"Come here, baby," her father said brightly, "Daddy'll hold you." He grabbed her up under the arms and she felt herself slung through the air. He pulled her close and she felt his heart beating against her back. "Stuffy," Jennifer said, and she slid off his lap.

"Did you hear that, Mother?" he said. He laughed but it

wasn't funny. "Our daughter's growing up. She said my holding her made her feel stuffy."

"Is that so?" her mother said. She sat still, listening. "*You're a part of this too*," he'd said. Part of what? Jennifer wondered. Of their love for each other and for her? Of this cheerfulness then and of the way Mommy looked at Daddy as though she didn't know if she liked him or not. She didn't want to be part of that, she wanted to be tiny again, to be nothing but eyes, ears, and skin, to be carried on the warm river of their voices, to rest under the moon and sun of their faces. Her heart thumped so loud she was certain they'd heard, that she'd given herself away, and she looked up, waiting to be discovered. But both of them were staring off in the same direction — past the hemlock trees and over the broken fence that marked the boundary of their yard.

"You know, believe it or not, Jennifer, Mom and I have discovered we have a lot in common over the past few months," he said. He spoke to Jennifer but he frowned at the back of her mother's head.

"What's *in common*?" Jennifer asked.

"*You*," her father said, and he dove at her. She squealed and ran, knees pumping high in panic until she was past the hemlocks, where she crouched and watched them. From there, they looked like two ordinary people — almost without faces, the way it used to be, her parents who loved her with a love that was vague and warm as the days she washed through dimly. But now, since her mother had gone away and come back, every time she looked at them she saw the lines around Mommy's mouth and the way it pulled down at the corners, and the crease that ran straight up between Daddy's eyes. She unfocused her eyes and tried then to make them those strangers whose soft hands and eyes spelled *love*, into whose midst she'd tumbled one day, a small stone from the sky. She would have liked to have been that way again. When she was little, they'd played a game that her mother called "Just Imagine." "Just imagine you aren't my parents, who would I be?"

"A little speck, a little girl speck."

"Would I have a name?"

"Only to yourself, one you made up."

"Would I be lonely?"

"Very lonely."

"Who would my parents be?"

"The wind and the rain."

"But who would I be?"

"Nobody."

And so on, round and round and back again. Without them you were nobody; with them you were who they were. Her mother lifted her heavy brown hair off the back of her neck. Her father swung and puffed his pipe. Under her breath, she commanded them to freeze, right there, to go no farther.

They froze. Her father's pipe smoke hung suspended and she was Jennifer the magical, Jennifer the powerful, and they would wait for her, she would make them wait until she caught up with them or they became themselves again, until they told her what was different now though nothing seemed to be, how this love that had taken her mother away and sent her back was the same (they said so) as what had created Jennifer in this world. Until they told her how this love they talked about pulled you apart and kept you together. Her mother slapped her knees and stood up. She pressed a finger to her lips and frowned and then she went inside. Jennifer ran back. "What are you and Mommy talking about?" she said.

"Nothing," her father whispered. "Have we been talking?"

"Not funny," she said.

"Not supposed to be funny," he said.

She was about to reply when she was struck by a wish, a wanting so potent she thought that if she could just have that one thing, she would be happy. She wished she could be the boy she knew in Hamilton who cut pictures of motors out of magazines and carried them around in a shopping bag, who could dump them out and explain them. All kinds of motors — washing-machine motors and the engines of cars, giant turbines and the tiny motors that drove electric clocks. He understood what they were for, he said only he knew why they worked, and all the children were afraid to make fun of him. She wished she could be that boy.

"You know Mommy," her father said, nodding toward the door where her mother had gone.

"Daddy, don't talk," she said. "Don't talk." She put her hand over his mouth. Startled, he grabbed her wrist. "Jenny," he warned. Then he seemed to remember, loosened his grip. "Mommy will be back," he said. "She's inside, she's coming back." Jennifer studied him, struggling to match another time with this time. Both times, Mommy was coming back and what was about to begin again was something fine, better than before. She remembered. He'd said the same thing at the bus station when Mommy had left.

He'd held her hand tightly that time too, so tightly the bones had crunched, and she'd understood then — Why, he's afraid. And then she'd been afraid too, afraid the way they said two people were afraid when they were drowning and grabbed onto each other until they both drowned. That day at the bus station, she'd tried to pull her hand away and she thought for one crazy second, as the lights began spinning overhead in small brilliant orbits and he'd loomed over her, that he might topple on her. The bus sighed, released its air brakes with a sharp rush. He looked down at her with his terrible forehead, his unseeing eyes, and he said: "Mommy's gone to collect herself, Jennifer, Mommy's coming back." At times like these, that terrifying picture returned: an exploding Mommy, then Mommy stooping, collecting herself, putting the pieces in a brown paper lunch bag, bringing the pieces home. Love did it. And now she was back. That was love, too. Someday they would explain. Later, Jennifer. Just have faith.

"I'm hungry," she said. The screen door slammed and her mother came out, drying her hands on a dish towel. "Me too," her mother said. "Daddy too. Just as soon as your daddy finishes cooking, we're going to eat."

Over the valley behind their house, the sun was setting in a swirl of blue and gold. It was the kind of sky that prompted her mother to sigh and declare their view the prettiest view in the world. Down below, at the beginning of the woods, where it was already dark, a gray mist climbed the wheat field. When the mist reached their house, Jennifer thought, night would begin.

When the hamburgers were done, she refused to sit on the ground. "Fine," her mother said impatiently, "then sit on the bottom step here and pretend we're on a camping trip and we're the only people in the world."

Jennifer shook her head no.

"O.K.," her mother said. "Just sit there and be stubborn then."

"Thank you," she said. She'd noticed that when people didn't want to do something, they became polite and then there was a fence around them that no one could cross.

They gave her a plate with the world's biggest hamburger on it. It was like a cartoon hamburger, the kind she ate with her father every Saturday at the drugstore: no onion, no mustard, a frill of lettuce, and the reddest red tomato. Twice she tried to bite into it, twice the bread slipped, and a pinkish mix of catsup and mayonnaise splattered onto her plate. It was the most beautiful hamburger in the world, but she couldn't eat it. She began to whimper. "Well, what is it?" her father said.

"Can't," she said.

"'Course you can," her mother said. Her father watched her mother but her mother looked at neither of them, just kept chewing her own hamburger in small fierce bites and staring straight ahead.

"Honey, you like hamburgers," her father said. "You've always liked hamburgers. I've never seen a kid cry so much over nothing, have you, Mother?"

"Yes," she said.

"Well for Christ's sake, what's she got to cry about?" he said.

"Why don't you ask her, you're the word man," her mother said. This was a joke between them: "You're the word man," her mother said when she wanted to tease him. "You figure it out." But she wasn't teasing now.

"I'll do just that," he said. "Jenny," he said. "Jennifer

Lynn. Stop that now and tell me what's wrong." But Jennifer couldn't stop. She was away and flying down a long in-drawn breath, taking in air to fill an empty place that seemed deeper with each breath, as though air had no power to fill it. Her mother knelt beside her. "Breathe," she said. "Jennifer, breathe." She clapped her daughter on the back and Jennifer breathed, wailed, and jerked her shoulder out from under her mother's hand. "It's too big for her," her mother said wearily. She rose from her knees like an old woman, first on one leg, then the other. "She wants you to cut it up for her," her mother said.

"Well, doesn't she know how to ask?"

"I don't know," her mother said. "Where'd she learn this trick? Who taught her anyhow? She didn't do this before I left."

"That's right," her father said. "What did you think, that she'd just sit here and wait for you, that she wouldn't change at all?"

"Right," her mother said.

"Right," he said. And the way they said it, *right* was a big engine that pulled a long black train out of a tunnel. You saw the engine and you sensed by the way it labored that it was pulling a weight, but you couldn't see, you couldn't, and you trembled against that seeing.

"O.K. then, love," the man said. He sounded tired too. Against the sky where the stars were backing away, his face looked worn and huge. When he picked up the knife, Jennifer shrank violently and flung herself sideways on the grass and cradled her head in her arms. "Well, Christ," he said. "Now what?"

She felt her mother kneel down beside her again. "There's

no reason for any of this, Jennifer," she said. She opened one eye and stared at the ground. She felt the earth against her belly where her shirt had hiked up and it was cool and damp as though in the ground it was already autumn. Her mother began to rub Jennifer's back in wide, smooth strokes. Jennifer felt drowsy. For the first time since her mother had come home she felt safe again, back in the darkness with nothing to do. Her mother's voice went on and on, gently now: "You've got a mouth," she said. "See." She pried Jennifer's face away from the ground and held her chin and pointed to her mouth. "See," she said. "You've got a mouth like my mouth and like Daddy's mouth. You can use it like we do and ask for things," she said. Jennifer rolled over. Moist dirt clung to her stomach, and the sky kept going away away away and below the sky, poised on the edge of the valley where in winter, when the green was gone, their exposed house looked so frail a hand could knock it down, there were only herself, her mother, her father, and the silence where the secrets of things lay hidden. She hated her mother's words then, hated the whole idea of needing or wanting anything, of having to crack that silence and ask and want, with a cold and definite hatred. And they called this love – what you needed and could neither ask for nor understand, what you closed your eyes and felt for blindly. She vowed to herself then, as solemnly as if she'd written the promise on a sheet of paper and dropped it into her secret place – the knothole of the basswood tree near the creek – never to want anything. Her mother searched her face and Jennifer stared back at her and, with the power of the knowledge of the new way she would be warming her, in pity and anger, she said: "*Your* mouth, Mother." And thought: That's a curse. When they said *"Don't curse,"* they meant what she'd just done, not the words but the feeling that caused the words. That was a curse.

Her mother grabbed the knife out of Ed's hand and chopped the hamburger into pieces and slapped the plate back onto Jennifer's lap. "Now *eat,*" she said. "Eat, I said, before you dry up and blow away." Jennifer relaxed. What a wonderful thought. What fun that would be, to become small and weightless, to catch every breeze that happened by.

"Well," her father said. "No long faces now. You can eat later," he said, and he scooped her up and carried her back to the swing.

"Ed," her mother said, "I just got her settled down, honey."

"Well, she's upset," he said. "She can eat later."

Margaret flung her arms in the air and gave up. Jennifer sneaked her thumb into her mouth and gave over to the drowsiness and the cool dark. She was too old to suck her thumb, but they wouldn't notice because they were talking to each other and rocking the swing. Softly at first, with wild chilly voices, the peepers chimed in over and around them, first in small groups, distinct chirpings from different corners of the yard, then louder, more unified, and soon the night was riddled with their noise. He said: "Not to change the subject, Maggie, but I saved something just for you because I know how you love those lakes." Her mother always said she loved the Finger Lakes because they were classrooms. She went on nature walks and bird walks and flora walks, saw Canada geese, loons, killdeer, heard the lunatic pheasants chuckling as they ran, followed the reedy marshes west and south and came home with a knapsack full of leaves, feathers, stones, and roots that Jennifer danced and begged to hear about. She said they each had a language. Her father winced at that. "Well, I have to have something that speaks to me that way," she'd say. "Someday," her mother would say, "you can go with me, Jennifer." Now Jennifer thought: The next time she asks, I will say "No thank you." She felt the satisfaction of that refusal as if it had already come true.

"Are you listening?" her father said.

"Don't I look like I'm listening?" she said. He shoved his face close to hers then and studied her. "Now that you mention it," he said. She blushed and bit her lip.

"Anyway," he said. "They took a sounding in the middle of Seneca Lake last month and guess what? There's no bottom to the damn thing, at least not one they could find. I have a newspaper clipping somewhere."

"Imagine," her mother said. "Must be an underground river or something down there, imagine that."

"Monsters," Jennifer said.

"No, no monsters," her mother said. "Creatures, maybe, but no monsters."

"Monsters," Jennifer said. Anything could be monsters, she thought. Sometimes the peepers were monsters. Sometimes it seemed they tried to shriek louder than anything around them. Once her father had been playing the stereo on a summer night much like this one. Her mother kept shouting at him, "Turn it down, turn it down." He pretended to misunderstand her — "You want it what?" — cupping his hand to his ear like an old man. The more she'd shouted, the louder he'd turned the stereo, the wilder the peepers had sung.

"You're quite some philosopher," her mother said gently. He looked pleased. He tucked his chin and beamed at her. They're trying to do something, Jennifer thought. They're doing it right now.

"Where does the lake go?" Jennifer asked. They looked at her blankly. She felt her face redden. Well, maybe once in a while you could want a simple answer, as long as it wasn't about you *personally*.

"Who knows?" her father said. "China, the center of the earth maybe."

"Oh no," her mother said. "The water would turn to steam at the center of the earth."

"Right," he said. "Only I wasn't talking about *really*, Margaret, remember?"

"At least you think," her mother said, as though pursuing some thought of her own. "At least you do that. A lot of people don't, you know. They're the miserable ones finally, don't you agree?"

"Oh I don't know about that," he said. "They may be happier, especially if they've never known much."

"I don't think so," her mother said.

"Well, if they don't know," he said, and a sly soft look came over his face, "how do they know they don't know?"

"I think you always know when something's missing," she said.

"You don't do so badly yourself in the thinking department," he said. He stroked her thigh with a faraway look on his face.

"Thank you," she said. She reached to tuck up her hair.

"You learned a lot while you were away," he said.

She folded her hands suddenly. "I learned enough," she said.

"Enough?"

"Enough," she said.

"Enough for what?"

The swing stopped and her mother stared at him. "I'm back aren't I?" she asked. She looked at him as though she were measuring him. Why did they talk this way? What was it for? Jennifer felt the boat, the way it had rocked the instant he'd said *"death do us part."* It was her mother pushing the swing again.

"O.K.," he said. "Don't get mad. I just want to know, that's all."

"It's too complicated," she said. "You don't want to hear right now. It's late," she said. "I'm tired and I'm not thinking clearly. Besides, don't command me that way, Ed. Really, I don't like it."

"Who's commanding?" he said. "Look, I'm happy. Look, here's to us," he said, raising his glass of water. "All right then, to us," he said again. "To us and to whatever you learned that brought you home."

"Stop it, Ed," her mother said.

"Do you want me to understand?" he said. "I just need to understand, that's all."

"Of course I want you to understand," she said. "Later. Let's just enjoy ourselves for once." Jennifer nodded. That was good. If she were in charge, they would just listen to the peepers and to the wind in the hemlocks. Because the longer you talked, the more you wanted to know, and then you had to go on. You turned into one of those people at Quaker meeting, always looking, always wanting something. Or you turned into Mommy and Daddy.

"Great," her father said. "Fine, great. I'll forget it. Remind me if I step out of line."

"Eat," her mother said, and she shoved Jennifer's plate back into her hand. Carefully, Jennifer began to peel the bits of hamburger free from the soggy pieces of bun and to set them in separate piles that did not touch one another. When she finished that chore, she picked off the tomato and lettuce and started to work on the catsup, squeezing the bun, scraping the goo with her thumbnail and wiping it on the side of the plate. She wanted to get down to the plain bun again.

Her father pushed the swing. Her mother pulled Jennifer close to her. She began to sing: "*Sweet and low,*" she sang, "*sweet and low, wind of the western sea.*" Jennifer's lullaby. When her mother sang, the wind blew across the western sea, that dim, milky sea, smooth as a brow soothed by a soft hand. Only tonight, when she closed her eyes and waited to hear the western sea, she saw the shore, and there were people walking up and down on the shore, turning shells with their toes, and the houses that lined the shore were brightly lit. She saw it as clearly as if she was there. She kept her eyes closed, trying to find that calm smooth place the lullaby always made, the cool place, smooth as a northern pebble. But it was no use. As her mother sang, the people walked up and down, in sunlight, on the shore of the western sea. Her mother's voice couldn't stop them.

"So come on, Margaret, could you tell me, please, what you meant back there about what you learned?"

"Whenever you care to listen," she said, "I'd be happy to tell you."

"What should I do, telephone first to make sure you're free?"

"Oh stop it," she said, "won't you?"

"No I don't think I will this time," he said. He stood up. "I don't think I will stop it just now. I think I'll hear what you have to say." He watched her as if he were having trouble seeing her, but he kept looking. Her mother sat still and seemed not to breathe. Then she clapped her hands. "Jenny," she said, "time for bed."

Her mother's hand stopped her protest. She'd been tricked. So this was where love took you, and happiness – it was some big secret that they promised, then took away. "No fair," she said.

"No fair is right," her mother said. "Now kiss us and go get ready for bed and we'll come up and kiss you goodnight in a few minutes." Her mother held her. She held her for a long time, and she let her go and then she held her again. "Don't slam the screen," she said.

Jennifer lingered in the kitchen, listening. "Go on, Jennifer," her mother said. "We'll be there soon." The burnished copper bottoms of the pots on the wall shone back at her and the quart jar of honey shone like congealed sunlight. She lifted the jar off the shelf and held it close to her face and tipped it so the pale gold honeycomb settled heavily to one side. She turned the jar slowly, trying to follow one cell all the way through the comb. She traced it with her finger on the outside of the jar, keeping her eye on that one cell, following until she came to the point where that cell met another and she lost the one she'd followed among all the others, all intricately, delicately, surely connected to one another. "Jennifer," her father called. "Are you dawdling?"

"No," she said.

"We're waiting," he said.

It wasn't like any going to bed she'd done before. It wasn't like being carried piggyback up to bed and it certainly wasn't like being lifted out of the car half-asleep and being carried up to her room so that the trip between the car and the room was lost in the warm blot of her father's body and the covers closed over her like warm water. That had happened to another girl. No, she was going on her own this time, toward the small blue night-light in the upstairs hall. And then her room opened in front of her, yellow and white, like summer — yellow toy chest, bookshelf, yellow-and-white checked canopy over the bed. And there was the windowsill, the ant farm, the turtle asleep on his rock under his plastic palm tree, and beyond the windowsill, across the ghostly fences, over in the dark, the ponies at the farm down the road still cropped grass. She was sure of it. And beyond the ponies and the grass and the last lights, to the east, there was Hamilton and her grandparents, dressed in their plaid flannel bathrobes by now, and beyond them, yet connected to them, the meeting house, gaunt and silent and dark now, and waiting. But below her window, underneath the slanted tin roof of the porch, her parents were talking. She couldn't hear them. She pressed an ear to the screen and listened. She thought she could almost make out their voices, low and quiet at first, then angry, sharp. Her mother said, "All right then, Ed, all right." And then he asked her something, he wanted something, and their voices dropped and there was only the keening of the peepers, going wilder and higher, spreading out, until the whole sky disappeared down the broad whirling throat of the sound.

Then the porch light went out. One minute the grass was white, the next it was dark. Jennifer drew back from the window. They were gone. She heard them come inside. They always said, "Jennifer's a brave girl." Well, she guessed she knew a little bit now about being brave, about why you had to be brave. It had something to do with the light's going out that way. It was because of love somehow, and because of what you wanted. You had to be brave, you had to wait and have what her grandfather said was faith, which was a special kind of waiting, a special kind of bravery and love that kept you standing in the dark, in the silence, looking for the light inside you, believing it was there.

She heard them start up the stairs. She jumped into bed and turned out the light. It was important that they should pick their way through her toys and books in the dark to find her. She pulled the covers over her head and imagined how they looked, coming up the stairs. They had their arms around each other. Her father's arms were dark and his shirt was white except where her mother held onto a handful of cloth at his waist. Soon they would stop at her door and see the mound of covers and catch on to the game and they'd say: "Well, where's our Jennifer? Who's that underneath those covers?"

"Let's call her, Daddy," her mother would say. And they'd call – "Jennifer" – they'd call softly, making their voices sound far away. And call again while they tiptoed across the room and she waited, shivering with excitement close to terror, for what was sure to happen. For the moment when they'd each take a corner of the bedspread and draw the covers back slowly and say, "Well, look who's here." For the moment when they'd pull back the covers to reveal — Jennifer the fair. She hid her face with her hands, to keep from them how it shone.

A Long Time Coming,
A Long Time Gone

ALICE HELD the eight-by-ten glossy photograph and looked into her own laughing face, at her flashing eyes and the hair tumbling in dark loose ways, at the fringed white buckskin shirt unbuttoned down to *here*. She took it all in. "Lord have mercy," she groaned to herself, smiling, "Will you please look at that?" It had happened in a moment, a flash had gone off, and the photographer had caught her, not as she was now, but as she would be, blossomed out into this joyful creature who laughed as though she'd just caught sight of the face of a loved one who's been a long time away. She picked up a skinny turquoise pen with a peacock feather coming out of the end and signed the corner of the photo. "Love ya," she signed in a hand as sleek and foxy-looking as the woman in the picture, "Alice Dyer." The 'r' trailed off into a musical note set with a star where the note should be.

Alice had moved back home last July after she had had enough of John Wallace Siddon, her second husband, and the running around they'd done on each other. They went through people so fast you'd have thought they were racing each other to find the ace in a deck of playing cards. Now, here it was, spring again, and outside the window of Alice's room, as usual on any day in late March in Memphis, Tennessee, her mother was walking around in the throes of her annual spring labor – preparing the flower beds for planting. She moved slowly, like an old animal walking a familiar path. She wore a pair of men's black high-top tennis shoes, black nylon socks, and a gray housedress with a handkerchief stuck under the belt. She was walking in the flower bed that surrounded the sundial, shaking some kind of white powder from a sack made out of an old net curtain and watching where it fell. If she missed a spot, she backed up and gave the bag an extra shake. Honestly, sometimes Alice wondered if her mother weren't rowing with just one oar in the water these days. "Hey," Alice yelled out the window. "What's that you're slinging?"

"Bone meal," her mother said without looking up. "Sweetens the soil."

That woman, Alice thought. You'd think she'd get tired of doing the same thing year after year. But never a spring went by that her mother didn't plant zinnias and marigolds and nasturtiums right back in the same beds where others of their kind had lived and died the year before. Even the spring Alice was twelve, the spring her father died, did his wife stop her planting? No, she did not. He hadn't been two days in the ground when she was back out there with her string and markers and packages of seeds, down on her hands and knees in the dirt again like nothing had happened. Never a spring went by that Alice didn't get restless all over again, watching her mother drop seeds into the earth. Or watching her sit out there of an evening as the season went on, with her hands folded in her lap and her face blank, as if she were listening for the first green shoots to pop up from under the dirt. Well, Alice had her own season. It started like spring – with a restless stirring inside tight husks and casings – but it wasn't spring, it was like two seasons – *always* and *never* – trying to happen at once. It began with a seed, a kind of hunger, and ended with a dream such as a seed might dream that never left the earth, as it lay in the ground and dreamed of its flower.

She pushed through the back door, letting it slam behind her, and stood blinking in the strong sunshine. The ground was lightly steaming where her mother had turned a new bed. "Mama," she called. "Now I want you to tell me why you go to such trouble when you'll just turn around and do the exact same thing next year?"

Her mother was back down on her knees again by this time, sifting it through her fingers as if, Alice thought, there could be a single clod or pebble left after all this time. Without raising her head she said, "Well, sure it's trouble, but, Lord, if you get to pick your trouble, I'll pick this." And she returned to her sifting.

Alice lingered until the strong smell of turned earth began to crowd so close to her she had to rush back inside and slam the window, get out the guitar, sit on the edge of the bed and play and play and play, every song she'd ever written until she felt like herself again and not like anybody's hungry child. This season, there was a special reason to practice and get ready – she was going to play a big folk festival in Knoxville, Tennessee. But even if she hadn't been, she would have gone on singing because singing was about the only thing she really wanted to do. She couldn't type worth a damn, never could stand waitress work, or clerking in a store, couldn't seem to stay married. But ever since she could remember she had had this voice and when she sang, Lord, when she sang, it felt like some answer was about to come to her to a question that she could never quite put into words, though all her life she had been asking it. When she sang she felt something coming that would change her and make her whole, something she'd been waiting for for so long she could almost taste it. And she felt that if she just kept singing and keeping watch, one day this thing would come to her and it would be full, it would be rich, it would satisfy the hunger and fill up the empty places and make her know why she was alive on this green earth.

The festival was held in a valley watched over by the blue presence of the Great Smokey Mountains. It was twilight when she went on stage. The audience knew her well from other times and places – a tall winter tree of a woman, dressed all in white: buckskin skirt and shirt with fringe on the hem and sleeves – and they knew where she would take them – down into the roots of that tree and up the long, bare branches stretched out against the sky. Finally, she stood like a statue – head bowed and her arm resting on top of the guitar – waiting for the cue to begin her last song. When the spotlight changed to blue, Alice came to life. She whomped down on the guitar, threw back her head, stomped the stage and started in on the song about freedom that she always saved for last because it ended things on just the right note. When she came to the chorus her voice broke free and soared off toward the mountains. "*Free as the rain that falls on the water,*" she sang. "*Free as the lonesome sky. Free as a child without any mother. Free as the years flying by.*"

In the audience, people closed their eyes and swayed against one another, while her voice took them places, and showed them things. It was a big voice, bigger than she was, and it came from someplace that was forever a mystery to her and the shadow of that place lay across it. Some people thought about a river, an old slow wide brown winding river, flowing in shade and then in sun. One person saw the shadow of a hawk cross a field of ripe wheat and disappear into a stand of pines. Another heard the whistle on a long train gone around the bend and out of sight. *"Free as the rain that falls on the water,"* Alice had made her way around to the chorus again. *"Free as the lonesome sky,"* she sang. *"Free as a child without any mother. Free as the years flying by."*

When the song was over and she opened her eyes, she saw the audience rising in one long wave that began in front of the stage and rolled all the way to the back of the amphitheater. They were standing up for her, and they were clapping and clapping. She blew them kisses and she felt calm and dreamy as though a soothing hand had been laid on her head. And then somebody struck a match, held it up. Then another, another, and soon the whole place was dancing with tiny flames. "Thank you," she said, "God bless you, thank you." She slipped down the steps and around back of the stage, through the hands that reached out to pat her, while the applause started again out front and went on in one continuous roar. And she stood there hugging herself, eyes shining with the light of those matches that had been held up to her as though they were lighting the way somewhere.

That's when a man – his name was Malcom, he said, but she thought of him as Good-Natured because of his sweet round face with the little features perched on it, like the face of the man in the moon — appeared out of the backstage crowd and took her hand. He was so serious and he stuttered so much she had to laugh as he told her who he represented — Mountain Laurel Records — and what and why and who — herself — and would she consider doing a record with them. Right here, right in Knoxville, soon? In April? "We've had our eye on you for a few years now," he said. "We're a small label, but we like to think we're a progressive label."

"You don't have to sell me, darling heart," she said, "I'm ready." She stood there after he was gone, holding the card he'd given her, watching dusk turn the mountains purple and thinking *it's coming now, it's almost here.*

Two weeks later, there she was, going through the door of the recording studio on Good-Natured's arm. The night was hers, that's what he'd said, bought and paid for so that she could make her record. He'd lived up to his name and had brought her a Mason jar, a half-pint of clear whiskey made somewhere back in the hills, tied up with a bright red ribbon. It was a gift you'd give to a star. And really, she guessed she was just about a star. Here she was in a recording studio, not a big fancy one, and not in Nashville or anything, but a studio just the same, with that tangle of cords and wires all over everywhere, the crushed coffee cups and music stands standing every which way, like everybody there had more important things to do than clean up after themselves, and a big control booth lit up like Christmas. Here she was, wearing her new red high-heeled boots, and the wide denim skirt cinched tight with a belt of Navajo silver, the white buckskin shirt with a bandanna tied at the neck and her hair brushed and brushed to the sleek gloss of a bay horse's mane. Here she was, sizing up the competition, the racks of albums out in the foyer beside the drink machine. A lot of gospel groups recorded in this studio, and their album covers showed sweet-faced women in long skirts and men with long clean jaws and sideburns, all gathered round the old rugged cross. She winked, poked Good-Natured in his soft stomach. "I'd like to make me a gospel album one of these days," she said. "Think I could pass for saved?"

"Well," he said, "I wouldn't know about all that."

She gave the whole bunch of albums a shove. Devotion always made her thirsty. She tossed her hair back and tore the red ribbon off the jar of whiskey, unscrewed the cap and took a nice long pull. It spread all the way through her, waking every slumbering appetite. She took another sip, another. And then the musicians were coming through the door and she was there to greet them and offer them her whiskey. "Travis Ferrell," Good-Natured said, "lead guitar." Alice curtsied and offered him a drink. She liked his bedroom eyes, his thick blond hair, the way that turquoise and silver bracelet nestled in the hair on his forearm. "Toy Lovett, he plays bass." He was dark as a foreigner. He liked her whiskey. "Bobby Sunday, he's your drummer." He looks it, Alice thought, fat and sloppy and with his shirttail hanging out. When he handed the jar back, she wiped its lip with her bandanna. "Cat Adams," Good-Natured beamed. "Best rhythm-guitar player in Knoxville," he said. "And twice Tennessee State fiddle champion." He had his hand on the shoulder of this little scrawny woman with black hair that stood up from her head like chicken feathers and about six earrings stuck through one earlobe. She was wearing a T-shirt that looked like a man's old undershirt, and black corduroy pants, and she walked right on in there like she owned the world, like she didn't care that she was little or skinny and she didn't need anything from anybody to fill her up or change her, like she had everything she needed right there in the guitar case and the fiddle case she carried in either hand. "I would shake hands," she said, "but my hands are full."

"That's all right," Alice said. "Don't feel like you have to." She took three quick sips of the whiskey. It burned all the way down and caught her up in its wild energy and spun her around. It was like celebrating with yourself about everything good that hadn't happened to you yet. Thirst made you do things like that, hunger did too, and Jesus had blessed them both. While they set up their equipment and tuned, she sipped and hummed and walked around and sharp spears of thought fired through her head like stars shooting down through the summer sky. She went out to the drink machine and got herself a Coke. She poured whiskey into it and stirred it with her finger, watching the ice dissolve. She ignored the worried looks Good-Natured kept shooting her. She knew the whiskey was for later, but when she was thirsty time might as well not exist and the world might as well be water because she was going to drink her fill.

She settled the earphones onto her head and hooked her heels over the rungs of the stool. The earphones were too tight, they pinched her head and made her ears feel hot and a sighing sound came through them that was like the sound of a radio station that's gone off the air. She was beginning to feel confined, hemmed in. That was not a good sign. They were all staring at her like sheep at a pasture fence, waiting for her to begin. She hadn't bargained for this. She didn't know exactly how she'd imagined, no, dreamed it would be, but it was something like a combination of the way she'd felt when all those people held up their matches and times when her father had come home and brought her something from where he'd been. Once, it had been a wooden apple with "Blowing Rock, North Carolina" written on the side, in gold. You opened it up, and there was another, smaller apple, then another, then another, smaller and smaller, until you opened the last one, which was tiny as a pea, and inside there was a real apple seed. She guessed she had hoped it might be like that.

"All right," she said, holding up a hand for quiet. "From the top," she said, ready to launch herself into the song that begged Jesus to take the pain of love from her life. It began with an announcement played on the fiddle by Cat Adams with such energy that it made the gooseflesh rise along Alice's arms. A woman of many talents, Alice thought, as she clasped her hands around one knee and began to sway. Then the bass slipped in and it was time – dum ah dee DUM DUM: "*Lord, to you I am crying,*" Alice sang, (dum DUM dum). Her voice made her nervous, coming back at her that way through the headset, but she recovered and went on. "*Here on your sweet earth below*" (dum ah dee DUM dum), "*Where you gave us sweet love for one another*" (dum DUM dum), "*But then Lord la la la la la la-la-la.* Get the idea? All right bridge, O.K. now chorus, *So call your love back home to hea-vun*" (dum dum), "*We don't know how to use it here below. Where . . .*" (DUM DUM DUM).

She snatched the earphones off and held them tight. "Wrong," she said. "Wrong, wrong. It's supposed to go softly there, pianissimo, right?"

"Alice," it was Good-Natured's voice, coming from the control booth. "Please don't yell into the microphone that way, Ronnie'd like to keep his eardrums." Ronnie was the engineer. She guessed he deserved to hold onto his eardrums.

"Sorry," she said, taking another sip of the whiskey. "I just get so impatient and excited. I'm just like a damn little kid on Christmas morning."

The lead-guitar player ran quietly through a scale. "Maybe if we had charts," he said.

"Oh, charts," Alice said, "I don't work with charts, love, I work with the feel of the whole song. I'm looking for that spark, see, I'm looking for that elusive something called chemistry." Good old whiskey, she thought, it made her strong as a searchlight's beam, looking here, there, cutting through the night with a diamond-bright light, signaling Here I am to anyone who might be watching.

"This is costing somebody a whole lot of money," a woman's voice said. "Do you want to spend it getting soused?"

Alice whirled on her stool and discovered, with a shock that magnetized all the sharp unruly feelings whirling around in her head and drew them toward a red hot center, that she loathed the woman behind that voice – Cat Adams with her fiddle and guitar, and the way she played, as though there was a note, one note, that might keep the world from blowing to pieces, and every time she picked up an instrument she had to find it again and play it. And it was her note too, you knew that by listening to her, nobody gave it to her, so nobody could take it away. Alice pointed her finger. Her nails were painted red to match her boots. "*Ms.* Adams," Alice said, "you want to keep your job?"

"It's your dime, Ms. Dyer," Cat said. "You spend it like you want to." She wiped the neck of the fiddle with a cloth that she took from her case and then she laid that fiddle in the case and put the cloth down over it as gently as if she were putting a baby down for its nap.

"You're wrong there," Alice said. "It's somebody else's dime, but brother I sure know how to spend it. Isn't that right?" She aimed her voice toward the control booth. She held out both legs and studied the toes of her boots. They were expensive Tony Lama boots, custom-made at the factory in El Paso, Texas. They had taps on the heels; each had a star on the toe. She'd bought them to wear dancing with somebody she hadn't met. They were so shiny that when the light shone on them she caught a glimpse of her face, a white shape with stars where the eyes should be, in their polished surface.

"Alice." It was Good-Natured again, standing up with his arms folded, looking stern as a judge. "Alice, could we please get serious here." He held up his wristwatch.

She sipped the whiskey, nodded, straightened out her skirt. I am serious, she said to herself. You don't know how serious I am.

"All right," she said. "Key of A again. For real this time." She closed her eyes and imagined that she was a magnifying glass gathering the rays of the sun and aiming them down onto her song. Sometimes that worked. Cat Adams saved the world with her fiddle one more time and Alice began asking Jesus to take the love that he had given back out of the world because people didn't know how to use it. It was good this time at first. The old excitement came back like it did every time she sang. Something was coming, everything in her leaned forward to meet it, like you would for the first glimpse of somebody getting off a train. She felt a smile waiting to bust out on her lips any minute. Then she began to listen to what she was singing and she felt herself falter. Something was coming, all right. It moved over the horizon and into sight. It was Jesus again, empty-handed as ever.

See, Jesus had let her down and he shouldn't have done that. She'd waited for him for a long time and then after she'd left Wallace, she'd found him and for a while everything was peaches and sweet heavy cream. But the thing that had finished it between her and Jesus had happened late one evening not long after she'd come back home, while she was swinging in the swing on the side porch at her mother's, reading scripture from the pocket-sized New Testament the Gideons had come around handing out door to door. This book had an alphabetical index of readings to turn to if you needed help with life's problems. "Adultery" came first (why is it that help always comes too late?), then "Adversity" and so on down through "Tribulation" and "Worldliness." In the section recommended under "Tribulation" she had come to the part about seeking first the kingdom of God and how everything else would be added unto you. That's good, she thought, and you know, it's true. Seeking was something she knew about for sure. Then she'd turned to the second reading listed under "Tribulation" and it was the one about how the kingdom of heaven is within you and when she read that, she slapped the book shut so quick she thought she might be able to forget that she'd seen it. She'd sent that book flying as far as she could throw it out across the yard. But what was written there had already taken root in her and nothing could tear it loose again.

Her palms had felt clammy then and her heart was knocking and pounding like a crazy something in a cage. She'd dragged her feet until the swing barely moved and she heard the creak of the porch swing and the rasping of the cicadas, she heard the bugs pinging against the porch light over her head, she smelled the river and felt its heat swarming all over everywhere. She felt the lonesomeness of every place that Jesus had vacated. Because if the kingdom of heaven and Jesus were all within, then he wasn't coming from anywhere and he wasn't going anywhere, he was just there all the time, died and risen both and it was up to you to know him both ways and from the inside out if you wanted to live in his kingdom. And so she guessed she wouldn't, thank you.

So she sang with a heavy heart, not about who Jesus was, or what love was, but about what they *weren't*. They did that song half a dozen times, a dozen. They went away from it and did a few more songs and then they came back and tried Jesus again, but her heart wasn't in it. Her heart was sitting right there like a good dog that's been told not to move until somebody comes back to claim it. Then Ronnie wound the tape back through the last few versions of the song and started it rolling forward again. The moment of truth, she thought, and she sat up straight to wait for it. All right then, let's have the moment of truth. Everything you did had one. Trouble was, it was never the right kind of truth, you could count on that. It brought no comfort and it didn't fill you up, not in any way. Her voice flowed out of the speakers and filled the studio. It was the sound of a person with a heavy heart trying her best to sound lighthearted. She tried for a joke. "Hold it," she said weakly, "Ronnie, honey, turn me off."

The tape rolled on and her voice went round and round inside her head as though it might go on forever, telling the same old story. If somebody wanted to drive me crazy, she thought, all they'd have to do is to lock me up in a room with the sound of my own voice to tell me what's what. She sat quietly then, listening, with a smile on her face and her hands gone to ice. "Lord God," she said to herself, "that's me." And she felt something coming again, only it wasn't Jesus this time, it was the emptiness and the stony stillness such as could have been felt in Jesus' tomb with the stone still over the entrance and no dawn coming. Then, mercifully, the song was done.

"No," she said. "That's all wrong. Not a thing right about it."

"Maybe one there that's worth saving," Ronnie the engineer said. "But that's about it." He flipped a bunch of switches up in the control booth. He was a small, quick, dark man with his hair pulled back in a thin ponytail. He jumped around up there like a monkey or something.

She had a brainstorm. "Ronnie," she said, "why don't we put some echo on that one? We could mix down the bass and throw on some echo and I bet it'd sound a whole lot better."

"Honey," he said, "I'm afraid a little echo isn't going to solve the problem here." His face was smiling at her, except for his eyes, which were sad. "Nothing to do but try it again."

"You know, there's not but one thing I can think of that's fun to do more than once," Alice said. At least she'd gotten the players laughing. Even old Cat Adams threw back her head and laughed. Alice slapped her knee and sipped the whiskey. Laughter was always good. It brought back a sense of perspective. She watched them over the rim of the jar, then held it up to the light. Half empty, she thought. Then she corrected herself, angrily. No, it's still half full. She pressed her lips together tightly for a moment and brushed furiously at her skirt.

"Sweetheart," Ronnie said. He stood up in the control booth and leaned into the microphone so he could see her and talk to her at the same time. He started counting on his fingers. "Loretta Lynn, Tammy Wynette, Crystal Gayle, Dolly Parton. I have worked with those ladies and every single one of them's willing to do a song as long as it takes to get it right," he said. "You're no better than them now are you?"

Her face felt like a big tin moon with a bright light fixed on it from someplace far away. Everybody was watching, waiting. "Well, darling," she said, "I guess I'm just in a class by myself."

"Shit," Cat Adams said. "Why don't we act professional about this instead of wasting time talking about echo and all that nonsense?" She was staring directly at Alice with those intense green eyes. The others studied their instruments, the ceiling, the floor.

Then Good-Natured was at her side, only he wasn't living up to his name anymore. His face was tight and flushed. "Let's get serious here, Alice," he said. He held his wristwatch up for her to see. 4:45.10, 4:45.11, 4:45.12. It was a kind that blinked the time, seconds and all, and beeped at you every hour. She felt relieved. When a man spoke to her sternly that way she felt as though a burden had been lifted off her shoulders. "O.K.," she said, in her smallest voice to let him know that she knew what was what. "Malcom," she said. "I need a few minutes here to pull myself together and then I promise I'll do what I came here to do." She crossed her heart. "Promise," she said, "I'll be right back. Now don't go away."

"Alice," he said. Her name sounded like a warning.

"Promise," she said, and slipped out through the door — safe. The sky was wide as an ocean you couldn't see across, restless with clouds and with the black shapes of mountains thrown up against the stars. It was the coldest time of night, the hour just before dawn, when all the warmth has escaped the earth and the sun has not yet risen to give it back. She began to walk and shake her head to clear it. Good old night, she thought. Good old walking. Good old whiskey and good old quiet stars, so far and so many it would take a person longer than two lifetimes to wish on every one. She tipped her head back and let the sky bathe her face, hands in the pockets of her skirt, swirling it around her legs. The stars on the toes of her red boots flashed as she walked. Now and then the moon flashed off the silver disks of her belt and made the white buckskin of her shirt shine, the wind went up under her hair and she moved along like a ship under full sail.

The longer she walked, the better she felt. She walked along the edge of the lot that paralleled the highway, then she turned and started back toward the mountain that rose straight up out of the earth just behind the studio. The air was colder there, as though even at night the mountain cast a shadow. Over in the east the sky was starting to lighten, which made the mountain look even darker. The closer she got, the blacker and higher it seemed, until it towered above her, blocking the sky. It looked like someplace God might have gone – colder than the earth, high, and darker than the sky, with the stars hovering above, offering light. But if God was up there, he was keeping real quiet and not letting on that he was any different from darkness itself.

She shook her head. You sure have some funny thoughts late at night. She walked out until she came to the highway again. Even at this hour a few cars came winding down the road between the mountains at the end of the valley, heading south, their headlights sparkling against the dark. Even at this hour. Good song title. Hum a few bars and I'll give it a go. She waved to a van with Alabama plates. It flashed its high-beams and went on down the road. She waved at an old Chevrolet bearing Tennessee plates. It slowed and stopped beside the guardrail and the man driving leaned across the seat and looked up at her. He was older than she and he had an open country face, brown and lined and soft-looking as a leather pouch turned inside out. In the back seat were three large burlap sacks with pictures of horses on Purina labels. The front seat of his car was clean, and a small whisk broom hung from the cigarette-lighter knob. A tray rested on the hump in the floor. It held a cup of steaming coffee and a sausage biscuit, with a bite taken out of it, on a McDonald's napkin. The radio was turned down low and an early-morning radio voice read the market futures for soybeans and corn.

She leaned over and caught a whiff of the inside of the car. It smelled of coffee and sweet feed and sausage biscuit. She had the queerest feeling in her body, as though all her senses and even her skin had roused up at the sight and smell of that car and that man. The feeling rose in her till she felt it coloring her cheeks and warming her scalp. It was a feeling of joy such as you'd feel when somebody you loved and who'd been away for a long time had at last come home. And it was as though while he'd been gone he'd had something of hers with him and now he'd brought it back. But what was it? Where was it? A map lay on the seat, a wallet, a little sprig of forsythia. When he saw her looking at the wallet, he moved it closer to him. Alice stepped back from the guardrail.

"Need any help do you, lady?" he asked.

She shook her head. "No," she said. "I guess not. I was just out walking, thinking some things through, you know. I was just waving to people, that's all. But thank you, though," she said. "You've helped me a lot."

"All right then," he said. He eased the transmission lever back into D and coasted back onto the asphalt and down.

Alice practically flew across the parking lot, she twirled and danced. Why, that man had given her hope again. Just a stranger, and here he'd come riding out of the night that way, reminding her of what she was about. The door banged back, startling them all. The guitar player had been sitting on the floor with his knees drawn up and his head resting on his arms. Cat Adams was stretched out on the floor with a book propped on her chest. Good-Natured sipped coffee out of a styrofoam cup and walked around. The clock on the wall said five A.M. She had only been gone for fifteen minutes. She clapped her hands and they looked at her, bleary and sour. The faces of the men were stubbled with new beards. God they were a ragged crew. She saw the coffee stains on the carpet, the old tired green color of the walls, the rips in the amplifier coverings, and Cat Adams's old scarred guitar with the wood around the pick guard gouged out. Why was it that everything in this world was bound to disappoint?

They climbed to their feet and she climbed back onto her stool and picked up the earphones and the jar of whiskey. "Now," she said, her eyes shining just the way they had shone when all those people lit their candles for her. "I'm going to tell you what I discovered on my little walk outside." She took a sip out of the jar. Up in the control booth, Good-Natured rubbed his forehead so hard that when he stopped his skin stayed red, as though he had a rash. She tucked her skirt around her legs. "Well," she said, "I discovered two things – the mountain and the road. Listen to me now. Those two things. We can climb that mountain, which means we can do that same old song over and over again until we wear ourselves out, or, now hear me out, we can trust to the road and what's coming down it. And who knows what we might find there?"

"So what's it going to be then?" Cat Adams said. She had the fiddle tucked up under her chin, plucking the strings and twisting the tuners.

"Well what do you think?"

"Eureka," the drummer said. He hitched up his pants and climbed in behind the drums. She tried to catch Cat's eye. Surely another woman would have to understand about wanting something so badly you didn't care what you did to get it, or who saw you. But that woman kept tuning her fiddle.

"We're going to do a number called 'Free as The Rain,'" Alice said. "Key of G. We'll run it through a few times so you know it and then we'll do it for real. It's easy, just your standard changes, G to C and then on the chorus it's D, G, A and so on. Got it?" she said. "Then here we go." She closed her eyes and swayed on her stool. She let them go through the opening chords five or six times, until the feeling rose in her again – something's coming, Alice, it's almost here. Then Alice began to sing. Cat Adams was smiling, eyes closed, sawing away on her fiddle. Then she let the guitar player have his say, and they were into the chorus. The bass was going like a heart beating time along its rough zig-zag way.

"Free as the rain that falls on the water," she sang.

"Free as the lonesome sky.

"Free as a child without any mother.

"Free as the years flying by."

She heard her voice coming back at her through the headphones. It was taking her down, like a seed toward the earth. She was going that way again. And she sang about that falling. Then she saw the country down below where she was going. It was a wide and stony place with one dark tree, a honey locust still locked in winter, standing up tall and throwing its shadow, so she sang about that tree and the shadow it cast. And when she reached the bottom, she looked all around her and she sang about the stone, she sang about the cold moon that shone there, in a voice that was clear and wide and dark as emptiness itself. Now listen, everybody, her voice said, I am going to tell you about a place I know. She sang about that place in a voice that rang off stone.

"Free as the rain that falls on the water," she sang.

"Free as the lonesome sky.

"Free as a child without any mother.

"Free as the years flying by."

She had had her say, She took off the earphones and laid them down in her lap and listened while the music came out of the headset, tinny and distant, like a radio playing two houses away. The others kept going, heading for home. They had made a circle and they were playing together. They spoke and answered with their instruments until the separate strands of what they were playing joined and became one song. Even the fat drummer whisking the snare with his brush knew the way. She felt a tenderness opening inside her, a kind of patience, towards whatever struggled to be born. It opened in her like a single wide flower. Then, with a flourish on the fiddle, they were done. They grinned at each other and the bass player bowed her way. She saluted them with her jar.

The only person not smiling was Good-Natured. "Alice," he said. He spoke as gently as he could, but she knew the news was bad. You just developed an ear for things, like the sound of certain footsteps or certain cars. Ronnie flipped switches up in the control booth. She slung her purse over her shoulder and picked up the jar of whiskey. There was a shallow film of liquid left in the bottom and she drained it down before she answered. She watched while it coasted toward her down the side of the jar so slowly she thought it might evaporate before it got there. It spread in her mouth like oily heat. She dropped the empty jar into the waste-basket on top of the red ribbon. "Umm?" she said.

"Well, that was a take," he said. "But, Alice, we don't have any more time here, honey. You used it all up."

"What'd I do with it?" she joked. Nobody laughed. She pushed through the restroom door. In the mirror she saw that the lipstick had worn off her mouth and her hair looked

limp and stringy. Her face had settled around its bones the
way it did when she was tired. She looked at the woman in
the mirror, the one who had sung about the emptiness and
felt a kind of mercy come to her after the emptiness was
done. She had the strongest desire to leave her face bare
that way, not to touch it, to go out of there wearing that
face, and all that it had seen, as her own, and to let other
people worry what they thought about it. That might be a
place to start. But the longer she stared the more she began
to believe that if she looked into this other woman's eyes
long enough, that woman would begin to speak, and when
she did, she would tell Alice things she did not want to
hear. She reached around in her tooled handbag until she
found a manila envelope where she'd stashed a few of the
publicity photos, just in case. She eased them out of the
envelope and looked into her laughing face. There you are,
she said.

She assembled her makeup supplies – foundation, blush,
powder, lipstick, eyeliner and shadow – on the washbasin
and started in on herself. Cat Adams came in and stood
looking at her with her narrow pointed face and those
intense green eyes, just like a cat crouched under a bush
watching a bird. "Look here," she said, "Malcom tells me
there may be enough there to do a forty-five. 'Course, they
don't usually do forty-fives, but in this case," she shrugged,
and mimicked Malcom's voice, " 'a definite maybe.' " Alice
held the mascara wand poised in front of her eyelashes. She
smiled at Cat. "Thanks, babe," she said. "But I'm an all-or-
nothing person." She put the finishing touches on her face,
and brushed her hair until it crackled and stood out around
her head. She put on her bright-red lipstick and blotted her

lips, tossed some cologne on her wrists and up under her hair.

"Now then, I feel better," she said, heading for the door. Then she stopped. "Something I've been wanting to ask you," she said. "Who gave you that name anyway? Who calls you that?"

"My husband."

"Oh." That's what she'd been afraid of. She looked at Cat and felt dizzy all of a sudden, as though she had become aware of some steady kind of motion, rolling like a tide, carrying everything and everyone toward something plain and true and terrible as a name that exactly fit. "Excuse me," she said. "I need some fresh air."

Ronnie locked the door behind them. The lock made a satisfying solid sound as it caught. At least that's done, it said. At least that's over. It was dawn. There was a leftover moon hanging on in the pale sky as though it didn't have the sense to set. They were all standing outside like a bunch of refugees, Alice thought, tossed off their ship. All except Alice. She felt the dawn on her face and she breathed deep. She felt that tenderness again, welling up inside her, toward all creatures and their weariness. She felt that she was going to be like this for a very long time. "Listen," she said. "You all look tired. You wait here, I'll go get the van." Good-Natured tossed her the keys.

She stepped quickly through the pale morning, listening to the birds, the traffic on the highway, watching the chimneys begin to pour smoke. A flock of redwing blackbirds descended onto a clump of cattails standing in a roadside ditch. They hung there swaying and calling to one another, in their clear melodious voices, ruffling their feathers and flashing the bright scarlet bars on their wings. Suddenly she was furious at them, sitting there like that, preening. There wasn't but so much beauty to go around in the world and it wasn't fair for birds to get so much of it. She ran at them yelling "Shoo, get out of here, birds," and watched them take off in a great confusion of wings until they were lost against the rising sun.

From somewhere up the valley, a rooster crowed. It was all right. She unlocked the van and paused with her hand on the key. In the shopping center across the highway, a Bunny Bread truck and a Sealtest milk truck were backed up to the front door of the Winn-Dixie. She heard men's voices, racks clanging, and saw the drivers wheeling hand trucks stacked with cases of bread and milk. She closed her eyes and breathed deep, breathed deeper. Quietly now, Alice, softly now. She could have sworn she caught a whiff of fresh bread drifting over the lot, invisible and yet full of comfort too, the smell of home and morning coming round. The mountains were still purple in the growing light, purple and silent and waiting for the light to strike them.

By the time Good-Natured dropped her off at the motel the pink and pearl-gray of dawn had vanished. Spring trees on the mountains stood up like pale green smoke and the sky was so pale it looked almost white. "Well, thanks for a lovely evening," she joked. His eyes, when he finally looked at her, were the pale, joyless white of that sky.

"I'm sorry you won't think about the forty-five," he said. "I'll come take you to the airport at three. Please be ready."

"You can count on me," she said. "I'm the best at being

ready of anybody you've ever seen. I am the champion of the world at being ready."

She closed her door and leaned against it, and for an instant the objects in the room left their places and seemed to float inches above the surfaces where they had rested, as though she'd surprised them in the act of running away. She closed her eyes and pinched the bridge of her nose and when she looked again everything had settled back down. She whipped the curtains shut against the brightening morning.

She undressed quickly, brushed her teeth, slapped cream on her face, and crawled between the sheets. She liked motels; motels were the best places in the world. Motels were like resting-places between two points: where you'd been and where you were going. And they had two double beds to choose from. You could pick either one and lie there on the crisp, almost cold sheets with the luxury of two pillows under your head and the sheet folded over the satin border of the blanket and your hands folded over the top of the sheet, thinking about things until you drifted off to sleep.

She looked at the photograph of her father that traveled with her everywhere and now sat on top of the TV. He was dark as an Indian, and his white shirt glowed. He had his foot up on the running board of his truck, and the truck was piled high with peaches. Up close, you could see leaves on some of the stems. Apples, turnips, peaches, pecans. He had hauled vegetables and fruit all over the Southeast and into Texas and he'd never worked for a soul other than himself until his dying day. He would go away, come back, go away again. She used to believe that he went away on his trips and backed his truck in somewhere and peaches and apples, turnips, pecans, onions, peanuts, and sweet honeydew melons tumbled into it right out of the sky. Then one time he stayed gone, and he was dead off the side of a mountain up in North Carolina, hauling a load of apples.

Sometimes, though, in times such as these, she felt as if he were about to turn up again, his truck loaded down with canteloupes from the low country of Carolina or pecans from the valley of the Rio Grande. He used to drive his truck right up into the yard and under the tulip poplar tree, and he'd call to her. "Come on out here, little sister," he'd call. "Climb up there and pick you out the best one you can find to keep for yourself." He didn't say pick out just *any* one, he said the best one. She figured that all her life she'd tried to do just that.

Oh, she knew he wasn't coming back, not *really*. She wasn't crazy (though sometimes she wished she was). She could just feel it in the air, and she would catch herself perking up whenever a truck went by, or a train late at night, blowing its whistle, or a barge on the river near home, sounding its horn. It seemed like those horns and whistles and wheels were saying something to her. Sometimes it seemed that the whole round world was speaking. Alice, it called, something's coming, Alice. It hooted and it moaned. A change is bound to come. Get ready.

Made to Last

THE CLOCK on the wall above the kitchen table is a smiling plastic daisy with a little pursed mouth, one round eye closed in a wink. Annie glares at the clock, knees drawn in close to her chest, her black T-shirt stretched to cover them. Watching the clock, drinking coffee, staring out the window at the lone pecan tree in her back yard and at her cat, a fat orange tom with one white foot, sitting beneath this tree, twitching as he watches squirrels rummage in the leaves. She's waiting for ten A.M. when it will be time to phone Stephen Augustus Marsh and give him the news. If this were my place, she thinks, that clock would be the first thing to go, followed by the formica dinette and four chairs, followed by the tired pink sofa and its dolorous matching chair, followed by the linoleum in the kitchen, and then the tight little hallway that leads from the kitchen back to the bedroom without benefit of a single light bulb. Followed by the pecan tree and the dried-up goldfish pond full of leaves. All things small, tight, old, dead, cluttered or grim. Out. What's needed here is order, grace, clarity, spaciousness. Step one. She picks up the receiver and dials the number of the phone in the trailer on the construction site where he works these days.

While someone goes to yell for Stephen, she hears the clatter of many hammers knocking. It's only a new job site she's calling, but lately whenever she's phoned, she's imagined that she's calling someplace on the frontier, a place where Stephen has gone to become a stranger, someone free to start over at who he will be. She wonders how they summon Stephen to the phone. With a wink and a leer? God, she hopes not. Hopes that one of the older men will bring him the message, someone who knows about the troubles that lead a woman to call a man at mid-morning on a workday, someone who'll rest a hand on Stephen's shoulder. A door slams. Footsteps. He's out of breath when he answers. "So when do you get here?" he says. "When can you get away?"

"From you?" she jokes. "Good question."

Silence.

"Stephen, listen, I've done it. I've filed the papers."

Silence.

"Well I don't like it," he says finally, "I don't think I want to hear that."

"You just heard it," she says, feeling her face turning to stone, thinking of the ways they align themselves these days: Annie – policewoman. Stephen – martyr.

"Look," he says, "I'm at work. I'm standing here covered with dirt. I hit my thumbnail when they told me you were calling – I'm watching it turn black right now – and you're telling me we're getting a divorce."

"You signed them," she says, her voice heading up toward that high edge she hates. "I mailed them to you, Stephen, and you signed them and mailed them back, remember? So we wouldn't have to serve you with them, so you wouldn't have to have the sheriff knocking at your door. Shit," she says. "I don't have to tell you what you did."

"Jesus, Annie." His voice is soft with sympathy. "Why is your voice so hard? What's happening to you?" She swallows that question whole. It sits in the pit of her stomach like a rock. That's what's happening to me, she thinks. "Annie, look. I didn't read them through, I couldn't, I'm not sure what they said. Could I see them again?"

"Stephen," she begins, eyes closed, holding the phone against her shoulder and pressing the palms of her hands over her eyes. See no evil, speak no evil. But no, those days are over. What he does, he does.

"All right," she says, "O.K., I'll mail you a copy."

"Well, actually, I thought you might bring them to me. We talk better face-to-face, don't you think?"

Silence. "Annie?"

"Yes," she says. "O.K. It's Saturday, what the hell."

"Jesus, Annie," he says. And she hangs up the phone, calls the cat in and feeds him — half a can, a whole can. He growls while he eats, swallowing whole chunks of food, then looks up, big-eyed, for more. "Aubrey, my sweet," she says, "it's never enough, is it?" He purrs, his eyes narrowed with pleasure, kneading the throw rug in front of the stove. On the way out the door she thinks twice, goes back and pours enough dry food into the dish to hold him until tomorrow. Just in case.

She's there by two o'clock, turning into the long lane that leads to the house between the Cherokee rosebushes that have gone so rampant they rake the sides of the car as she passes. As usual the house surprises her. There is something sullen and stubborn-looking about it. Though it is wide and two stories high, it seems hunkered down and morose back there in the hickory grove, with the porch's broad tin roof pulled down low as Stephen's cap when he's angry. Stephen has set a pot of geraniums out near the front steps. Their red blooms stand out against the brown, unpainted wood. Stephen isn't home but the house stands wide open. "Welcome," reads the heavy jute mat outside the door. Bunches of dill tied with brown twine hang from the porch ceiling, unmoving in the still heat. A walking stick carved from a hickory limb leans against the wall beside the door. Not on your life, Annie thinks. Stephen might come back and find her inside, and since for Stephen seeing is believing and anything can be a promise, he might think she has come home. Which I have not, she says to herself, looking in the front window nearest the door at the green couch, the Oriental rug she left behind, her muslin curtains at the windows, and don't you forget it.

A year ago, in this same house, her mind made up, she'd packed everything she owned, carefully, slowly, as though she were wrapping things for posterity. Until the end. Then she'd dropped a green glass bowl, a treasure, and when it broke it let loose a storm of noise. Cups shattered, doors slammed, coat hangers rang in the closets, pan lids rolled like giant coins across the kitchen floor. She had been in a blind panic to get away. And just at the moment when she was forcing the trunk down onto her winter clothes, Ellen, one of Stephen's students at the high school, had appeared, gliding down their lane in a long red Buick convertible. Ellen – a vision of delight, with big blue eyes, crinkled hair, tiny red-satin shorts, and a tube top that hugged her tiny little breasts – had popped out of the car, a sheaf of lavender paper clutched in her hand. Annie had groaned. Wild-eyed, Stephen had grabbed the paper. "Jesus Christ," he'd shrieked, "will you get the hell out of here?" While Annie sat rigid as a stick behind the wheel of her car.

"More poems?" she'd asked, snapping her cigarette out the window, veiling and hooding her eyes.

"Annie, it's not that way, really, look, see." As she'd backed up, turned around, pointed the car down the lane, he'd followed, staying close to the window so she could see how he was tearing the lavender sheets of paper into tiny shreds, a look of maniacal concentration on his face, how he was throwing them into the air for the wind to catch and scatter. As she'd tailgated Ellen down the lane, leaning on the horn, a kind of noisy funeral if anyone had been in the mood to appreciate it, he'd trotted along beside the car. At the end of the lane, when Ellen had peeled off onto the asphalt, Annie had stopped and bowed her head onto the steering wheel.

"I know you're not messing with her," she'd said. "I know you're just flirting, that's not why I'm going."

Stephen had leaned in the window. "Then why?" he'd said. "Why are you going? Is it really such a matter of life and death if you can't even tell me why? I need you, Annie, you need me."

At the sound of that word, fear had struck her like a flash of light. But she wasn't about to be detained to go into it again. Besides which, the fact was she couldn't *say* just exactly why she was leaving, because she wasn't leaving for one reason or many reasons, she was leaving because of, well, because of everything. But he'd looked so awful, standing there, as though he were freezing to death right there in the heat of the day. So – "It always zig-zags out of control, Stephen," she'd said. "No matter what we try and do, we never get it done. That's all I know, I'm sorry." She'd pulled out onto the highway, it was one of those moments when looking back might turn you into a pillar of salt or stone and yet she couldn't help it – one quick look in the rear-view mirror – and there was Stephen, tearing up clumps of grass, weeds, grabbing anything he could get his hands on, throwing it all after the car. Oh Lord.

Now she's back. Ellen has gone on to college. Stephen has quit teaching. Annie has stopped smoking and she's back, and Stephen rounds the turn at the end of the lane on his motorcycle, carrying red roses like a torch above his head. He's wearing his newsboy's cap pulled low, the one with the silver R.A.F. wings clipped to the upturned bill. Damn, Annie thinks. Damn if that isn't just like him. And it seems that everything she knows and loves, everything good about him, is there in the way he steers for the deep sand, holding the roses steady, and guides the bike through, shifting his weight right, left, steering it with his whole body. Damn if he isn't something else. And damn if I wouldn't like to pick up that glimpse of him and weave it like a thread into that cloth we tried to make – this one gold, that one silver, this one green – till pretty soon we'd have a whole blanket for the both of us to lie down under. Then the roses are dumped in her lap – "Well, Stephen," she says, "well, thanks" – and his face is so close to hers she can see the layers of brown that make up the brown of his eyes. "My love," he says, "been waiting long?" He's wearing a white cowboy shirt with pearl snaps and blue and green bucking broncos embroidered on the chest; he's wearing Army-green shorts and combat boots minus socks and laces. His hair is wet under the cap, curling a little at the neck, plastered to his forehead like a dark shingle.

"That was last year," she says, "you must have me confused with somebody else."

"No, not me," he laughs. "I don't confuse those things. So what brings you this way? Nice dress," he says, before she can tell him what brings her this way, as if he didn't know. "Blue," he says, "is definitely your color."

He steps back and whacks the nearest tiger lily off its stalk, while she sits there, nonplussed and unblinking, hating what she has to become sometimes in order to weather his stubborn innocence. But what else is there to do around Stephen, whose life is like this house and yard, everything rank, overgrown, sweet, choking on its own lushness? Where nothing ever holds or builds, and the only things that carry on from season to season are the wildflowers and the bulbs gone wild — Carolina lilies balancing their yellow turbans on thin stalks, blue-eyed grass and daffodils multiplying so fast the yard is choked with them. Where survival is a matter of being wilder and stronger than your neighbor, scrambling over the thing growing next to you in order to live.

This had been their third house in as many years of marriage. It was in the Piedmont, near Greenville, South Carolina, where you could stand on the front porch and see the mountains rising up out of the flatlands like a long blue wall. He'd found it on that trip he'd made up from the coast to interview for the teaching job he finally accepted, and when he'd described the place to her, he'd made the yard sound like a garden and the house a calm center to this storm of day lilies and hickory trees and Cherokee rose. But when they'd moved, she'd found a house so fly-specked, cobwebbed, mouse-tracked, nested-in, and gnawed that she wasn't sure that they'd come to the right place. Looking at the smudged windows, the yard full of broken limbs, thistles, high grass, she'd had that first claustrophobic sense of seeing through Stephen's eyes, seeing through the present and clear on into the future, seeing a place that hadn't been built yet.

Stephen had wanted to move right in, to live in it as though it were already the place he had described. But then, for the first, the only time, she'd insisted. She thinks of those first few months when they'd wake up at dawn, refreshed, strong, ready for work, and how that work had steadied them. They'd washed and polished and freed the place from its coating of dust and bug carcasses until the house resembled the place Stephen had first described. Until it became again a house that was fit to be handed down. Till the windows were clean and allowed the sun to follow its daily path through every room, the way it had been planned. Till the pine floors gleamed, and underneath the floors, she swore she could feel the floor joists, heart pine timbers four feet through the girth, bearing her up wherever she walked. Till the smell of sun-warmed pine surrounded them, and she'd felt they might have gone anywhere from that point, making of this life between them a room swept clean and set right.

And now, to break the silence that has fallen across the porch like the shadow of one of the hickories, she asks

"How's business?" She shifts the roses from the crook of one arm to the other. Stephen is swinging the walking stick, taking aim and knocking acorns and sticks out into the yard.

"Great," he says. "We're doing a split-level for a dentist, should make a couple of thousand each." He'll never go back to teaching, she knows, not as long as he can toss around phrases like "a couple of thousand each." "How's the book business?"

"Better," she says. "I'm assistant manager now. I still work long hours, but it's getting better."

"Assistant manager," he says. "No wonder you look haggard."

"Stephen, honestly," she says, irritation stinging her like strong sunlight in her eyes, "you say the nicest things." She thinks of the woman she'd seen in the mirror that morning, the one with high color in her cheeks, who'd sleeked her hair back and plaited it into one long chestnut braid. Haggard? "Well if I look haggard, you look thin," she says, twiddling the end of the braid.

"I have had things on my mind other than food."

"Oh, Stephen, stop it. This is serious," she says. She wraps her arms around his waist and presses her head against his chest.

"You're telling me," he says, kisses the top of her head. "Well, come in, come in," he says, shaking himself loose and swinging back the screen door. "I've got a surprise for you."

She balks, wary again, used to Stephen's surprises, his reversals and changes of direction. "Come on, come on." Take a deep breath, Annie. Over the threshold and down the hall. Don't look at the old sheet music and flags thumbtacked to the walls, the little dried weeds and wildflowers in every stage of decay stuck in glasses of cloudy water. Wherever Stephen is, there lies chaos, one short step away. Out the back door, his surprise is waiting. The L-shaped back porch is framed in new pine two-by-fours. Soon, he says, to be a greenhouse. She slips the roses into a Mason jar and sets them on the porch railing. "Your first plants," she says. Then bites her lip, thinking of all the growing things he will have there and how it would be to watch them take root, sprout and grow — morning glories, sage, tarragon, the feathery pungent dill, defying winter, coming into their own right outside the back door. Imagine.

"Anyway," he says, "that's all yet to come. Let's go fishing."

"You're on," she says, relieved. The pond across the road is one of her favorite places. She dreams about it sometimes, the waving cattails that line the banks, the trees in full summer lacework, the water changing as the light shifts from a muddy shade of coral, like tea cut heavily with milk, to the gold of a gilded pool. They come to an opening in the cattails, a small trampled beach, where the sharp, cloven tracks of deer, the claw-tracks of coon, mingle with footprints, as if this is the place where everything comes back to drink. "Where are you taking us?" Annie asks, stepping into the rowboat.

"To a hole where the fish hide out on hot days," Stephen says. "If you find it, you can pull them in all day and half the night."

She studies his face for a sign, a twitch of the lip, the lowering of one eyelid. Is he joking? "No, really," he says, "I'll show you."

This makes Annie catch her breath, because if such a hole exists, Stephen is the man to find it. There aren't too many men in this world, she knows, who would even admit that they believed in such a thing, much less set out to find it. He rows from the bow without turning to look where he's going, with that serious expression on his narrow face that makes him look like some fine-boned dark child, and she wants to reach over and touch him everywhere — touch the small scar beside his mouth, the blunt tips of his fingers, and then the anger rises again and she wants to shake him instead for everything he promised, for everything he cannot do or be. There was a song he used to sing to her when he was first learning to play the guitar. He has a rich grumble of a voice and he'd sing: "The water is wide," he'd sing, "I cannot cross over." She would lean real close so she could *feel* the words. "Neither have I bright wings to fly. Build me a boat that can carry two, and both shall row, my love and I." Well, they couldn't even build the damn boat, much less row it, and now here they are again, Stephen rowing and Annie in the stern, and then he glides into a cove and dips the oar in one sure backstroke. The boat rests on the water, floating easy as a leaf, his line is over the side, and sure enough, before the ripples made by the sinker have reached the shore, Stephen hooks a fish.

"See," he grins, "I told you so," pulls up a bluegill and drops it into the bucket at his feet. "Want to see me do it again?"

"Sure." He casts, whistles, looking at the sky, the bobber goes under, the bluegill comes up, flapping. "Satisfaction guaranteed."

With each bright fish that comes out of the water, Annie feels gloomier and gloomier. All around, on the shores of this pond, are other houses like Stephen's – tall and gaunt and plain among their groves of trees. Stephen casts and waits and a bad spell settles over the place, sends the fish into hiding, brings the sun out from behind a cloud to glare on the water, sends them drifting into a mat of water-weeds where Stephen's line tangles. He yanks at the line and stares off toward the shore with a set, gloomy look. In the yard of one house, someone is moving – a woman – bending, lifting laundry out of a basket, hanging it on a line. It flaps and glares in the sun.

"Whole families live there, Annie," Stephen nods toward the shore. "Generations have lived in some of them. Think of that. They must know every mouse-hole and chink in the firebrick. They don't give up," he says. "They don't – oh, what is that quote – They don't 'alter when they alteration find.'" He looks pleased with himself. "That's it," he says, jiggling the line to free it from the weeds. "They don't 'alter when they alteration find.'" He smiles a little smug smile.

"No, and I'll bet they don't go out looking for alteration either," she says.

"I suppose not," he says, and he looks so stricken that were this another story, she'd go to him across the rocking boat and they'd fall into each other's arms and forgive and forgive and forgive. But he looks at her instead, his eyes gone bleak, narrow and dark, and he says "What about those goddamn papers you've been so busy drawing up?"

She's conscious of the bottom of the boat just then, how fragile it feels, how the water slaps against the soles of her shoes through the thin wood.

"Yes," she says, "I've filed them because you weren't going to."

"That's right," he says. "That's the difference, one of them, between you and me. I don't give up," he says. "And you do."

What he says lodges in her chest, heavy and tight. Only noise will work it loose. She stands up in the boat and yells: "LISTEN EVERYBODY, WHATEVER IT IS, I DID IT, IT'S MY FAULT." The sound ricochets off the trees and hills and houses surrounding the pond. The woman hanging laundry waves to them. And Stephen lunges for her while the boat rocks, grabs her wrists and says, "Just sit down, Annie. Just stop yelling like that and sit down."

"Let me go," she says, "and I will."

"All right then."

"All right."

On the way back from the pond, they take the path through the abandoned peach orchard, a dry hillside where the trees are planted in terraced rows. The ground there is cut into dried furrows. It looks hard, tight, mean and unforgiving. It looks, Annie thinks, as though they got one chance, they plowed it once when the ground was moist and then it never rained again. Kudzu has overtaken some of the trees at the bottom of the hill and changed them into green mounds. Higher up the slope, the trees are bare and wounded, stripped of all but a few clusters of leaves and peaches so hard and dry they look as though they've been nourished on the clay-colored summer dust and watered by the white summer sky. But to Annie this might as well be Eden, a place where you see in every ruin a chance to begin again.

I could do something here, she thinks, following Stephen down through the trees on the path he's made going back and forth to the pond. I could learn what steps to take to salvage what is left here and make it thrive. She lets him go ahead and stoops beside one of the trees, digs her fingers into the hard clay, loosening it from around the roots. Like that, she thinks. That would be a start.

Back at the house, fish stored in the refrigerator, they circle each other, checking the clock, the lowering sun. It's too early for dinner, too early to start talking, else they might end up hungry. No, she thinks, it has to be after dinner; that's the time that has been set aside for things like this since people first began to speak to each other.

"Let's get out of here," she says. "Take me somewhere. Let's go get lost."

He's up and ready. "You're on," he says.

He's proud of his truck, a fierce old green International Harvester with a cowcatcher bolted to the front grille. He'd bought the truck in the same shape he bought the motor-cycle — both hopeless wrecks — both now restored to mint condition. Give me time, he says, and I can fix almost anything. He ushers her into the cab of the truck with a low bow, then ushers her into the liquor store where they buy a cold bottle of Blue Nun wine and, for a joke, two long-stemmed plastic wineglasses, one with *Bride*, the other with *Groom* spelled in white script around the cups.

The road runs through fields of crops that have been ruined by six months of drought. Seared ears of corn press tight against the stalks and the corn leaves are as brown and withered as if this were October, not July. Field after field of yellowed beans, brown corn, cattle standing in the paltry shade of tulip poplars or hip-deep in the shrunken ponds. They drink the wine from the cups at first until they can't think of any more jokes to make about them, then switch to the bottle, passing it back and forth. Stephen is talking about the drought. It has been so long and brutal, he says, the pines are dying. Even their long taproots cannot find water. Then he's talking about what could be done, what should have been done, what *he* would have done, to help the farmers salvage some of their crops. His talk falls like rain on the ruined fields. Rain, rain everywhere. You can almost see the fields turning green again below his talk.

"Stephen," she says, taking a long cool sip of wine, "did you see those little tiny peaches on one of those trees back in the orchard near your house? How do you guess those trees survive and make peaches in this weather?"

He stares at her, shaking his head. "What I will never understand," he says, "is why you see everything in such a depressing light, Annie. It can't be good for you."

"I'm talking about how they survive, Stephen," she says. "That's not depressing." Survive, she wants to say, don't you hear me? Stephen, let me tell you what I mean. Then you tell me what you mean. And maybe we can make another kind of survival out of what you know and what I know. God, she thinks, watching the road come toward them, I wish you had slept with Ellen. I wish you had slept with every one of them, or that I had run off with your brother or something. I wish things had happened that we could point to and total up and say: See, this is why I cannot be with you any longer. This and this and this. "Never mind. Forget it," she says. She leans back into the seat, shuts her eyes. It's nice just to let go, to let your head roll from side to side with the motion of the truck, nice just to drive and feel the heat coming through the window and drink the wine and be quiet.

The blast of an air horn strikes them like a wave and she opens her eyes in time to see the front grille of a semi disappear out of the driver's window as Stephen yanks their truck back into the right lane. "Stephen," she speaks so quietly he must lean over to hear her. "You can be reckless with your own life but please, will you leave mine alone?"

"I thought that's what you came here to make sure of," he says. "That we'd be leaving each other alone from now on."

"Right."

"Right."

She snuggles back into the seat and closes her eyes — you're trying to get lost, remember? — and doesn't open them again until the truck begins to lurch and bounce from side to side. They're traveling down a rutted clay road flanked by young pines planted in even rows. Stephen drives too fast, as usual, with his wrists draped over the steering wheel, as usual, so it looks as though he's not steering at all. His foot never touches the brake, her eyes never leave the road — steady, Annie, she thinks, keep your hand off that door handle — until at last they rattle into the bare clay yard of a half-finished house and he hits the brake pedal so hard the truck slides sideways and stops with the cowcatcher two feet from the trailer, the same construction office she'd called earlier this morning. "Bravo," she says, waving the wine bottle. "Nice driving, cowboy."

"Thank you," he says with a bow.

The house is three tiers of framing and a half-finished roof covered in tarpaper. It looks, Annie thinks, like a model of a house made of popsicle sticks. How does a person come to know how to build a house? she wonders. How to support it, how to make it solid with sheetrock and floors and a roof. She envies Stephen the chance to learn. She walks through the rooms, admiring the two-by-sixes, picking up tin disks and shavings that litter the floor. She climbs the makeshift stairs onto the plywood decking of the second floor, looks out through the roof beams at the high hot clouds.

"Cathedral ceilings," Stephen scolds from below. "Isn't it amazing the names we tack onto things? This house not only has cathedral ceilings, it also has a great room and a wet bar." He looks so funny, she thinks, so earnest, the R.A.F. wings shining on that cap as though any minute he were going to fly away from wet bars and great rooms, fly out through the cathedral ceilings and straight on up to heaven.

"Stephen, you know what?" she says. "I'll tell you the truth. At this point, I'd settle for a house like this, cathedral ceilings and all, I really would. At this point, cathedral ceilings don't look so bad to me."

"Annie," he says, "I'm shocked. You don't mean that."

"Yes," she says. "I do."

"I'm coming up to see you," he says. "This is serious." He starts up the stairs. "I can tell you need a good talking to. I can tell by the way you're smiling at me that you want me to talk you out of all this foolishness."

"Stephen," she laughs. "It's no use."

"Then I'll just keep right on going," he says. And he

climbs a ladder that pokes up through the open roof. Then he's up on the roof beam, balancing. "See," he says, "this is what I do, and I do it well. I'm up here, see, someone hands me a piece of plywood and I walk with it over to here," he balances, walking along the beam, carrying his imaginary sheet of wood. "I walk over here and I nail it down, see. Then I walk back and get another piece. That's what I do all day long. I can tell you what's out there to see for fifty miles around. I can tell you how many nails go into a sheet of plywood to join it to the roof. Then I jump down." He jumps, lands hard. "And still I don't fall. I don't falter. I walk over to my wife and then what happens?"

She holds his face between her hands and kisses him with a fierceness that startles them both. He kisses her back. She presses against him and kisses him some more and then they're lying on the plywood floor kissing and holding each other and she is loosening his belt and he is working her dress up over her hips. She feels him under her hands again, the small of his back and his shoulder blades and she's going under, down, back to that place where they just might start all over again, back to that first and best chaos when it didn't matter where they were, and who they were was something they had forgotten and found again, each time calling "Move over, make room, where are you? Come in, come in."

Only this time it's wrong. Stephen's weight on her, his mouth, his hands, there is something holding their bodies apart, she can't go under. His mouth feels cool and dry, his hands as light as dry leaves brushing her, no conviction in them, and no desire. She opens her eyes – nothing but the white-blue sky and clouds sailing over the open roof and the long shadows of the spindly pines reaching across the floor. Nothing over them, nothing under them but plywood decking and sawdust shavings. He's looking down at her, stroking back her hair. "I'm afraid," she says. "Stephen, I don't feel safe here."

"Afraid?" he says, "Annie, you?"

"Yes," she says, "Afraid, Annie, me. Yes to all of those things."

Now, it's dark. They're home again. The house seems to shrink back from the headlights as Stephen wheels the truck into the yard. He kills the engine and the lights, and they sit in the cab listening to the ticking of the engine as it cools, to the crickets and the cicadas, the steady sound of the motor that drives the water pump. "We didn't get lost, did we?" Stephen says, scratching at a bare spot on the steering wheel, breaking the silence they'd kept throughout the drive back to his house. She shakes her head no. "What'd you say, I didn't hear you."

"I said no."

"In that case," he says, "I'm going to pick us some wild greens for supper." He yanks the headlight knob and he's out of the truck and walking, hands in his pockets, studying the ground, stooping now and again to tear something from it. She remembers the time when Stephen left for a few months, back when things started getting crazy, after they'd been married for a year. Left to get his balance, he said. Drove around for two months, camping in all the state parks. He'd told her later about parking one night beside a river and how he'd woken up in the morning to find the car mired in mud up to the wheel wells, and how, instead of walking out and getting help, he'd waited there for three days while the mud dried. Same song, she thinks, last verse. Stephen passes through the headlights again, holding something in his hand, his chin jutted out, the cap pulled low. While she sits with her fists clenched on her knees, watching him. This is what I love in him, right here, right now, she says to herself, whatever cannot be made a part of any other life, not even a shared one. And I have to look, I have to know, because it's important not to leave without knowing what you love and who you're leaving, or else the next time around you might make the mistake of believing that you can love only what you do not lose.

She jumps down from the truck, runs inside the house and down the hall, snapping on lights as she goes. *Hurry, this is the last possible hour.* In the kitchen she rummages through the cabinets until she discovers the frying pan. She works fast, as though she has to get it all ready before Stephen comes in and upsets everything. This is silly, she thinks, but she turns the flame under the pan on high anyway, tosses in butter and rosemary, stirs it around. Why is it that around Stephen, everything a person does seems like a salvage operation: you only get to keep what you've managed to rescue? Then Stephen is there, holding a double handful of greens. "What's the big hurry?" he says.

"It's late," she says, "I need to be getting on home."

Stephen prepares fish the same way he does everything. Scales fly, falling in a shower onto the drainboard. He whacks off the heads, splits the bellies, reaches in and pulls out the entrails with one sure twist. He reaches under the counter and pulls out a bottle of sherry. "Here," he says, "I was saving this for a celebration but this is as good a time as any." Good sherry, too, none of that cheap stuff.

Isn't that just like Stephen? He may live without electricity sometimes but he will not be without his bottle of sherry, to cook with or to drink. He doesn't skimp, he never holds anything back.

In the middle of these preparations, the telephone rings. Stephen answers, the knife held up toward the light, glistening with scales. "Guess who's here?" he says, and Annie groans. His parents. She shakes her head no, no don't tell. "That's right. No, just for this evening, I think. Want to talk to her?"

There is nothing to do then but to take the receiver and talk to his parents. She had hoped to get away without doing this, to get away with the recollection of their affection for each other as something like a free-flowing stream that has never been dammed or reached the ocean, that has kept flowing on and on. "Oh, just cooking dinner," she answers. "How about you?"

In the silence that follows their two answers Annie hears the TV going in the background. "What're you watching?" she asks.

"It's Saturday," his mother says.

"Lawrence Welk," she guesses. Daddy M. chuckles from deep down in his chest.

"Annie," he says, "do you think there might be a chance of your getting down this way anytime soon, you and that son of mine?"

She bites her lip. "Daddy M.," she says, "I'm afraid not." Stephen dumps all the greens into the steamer at once and water splashes over onto the burner with a hiss. And she thinks of the kitchen chair pulled up under the hickory in the back yard down at Daddy and Mama M.'s. The chair and the card table covered with a dark blue oilcloth where Daddy M. sits in warm weather, taking apart his fishing reels, oiling them and putting them back together. And those tiny gears and pins and wheels, spread out like stars in the sky, if they could be counted, would yield the sum of what has been lost, of what she will miss.

"Well," he says, "we don't like to hear that."

"Mama M.," she says, "Daddy M.," as though she can taste their names, "I don't like to say it."

Stephen takes the phone again, says "Now, Mother," then more sharply: "Mother. All right," he says, "all right. Yes, sure. 'Bye." He throws the receiver back into its cradle, shakes his head once, hard.

"Let's eat," Annie says. She touches his back — "Stephen?" He leans against her hand, then pushes away. She works a fish loose from the pan, skin and all, for Stephen. He heaps the plates with greens. The greens have a taste that she can't place — wild as though the earth is in them. Stephen mops his plate with a roll, sops up all the grease until there's just the milk-white spine of the fish with its upcurved ribs left on his plate. Then he scans her plate.

"Now look at that," he says, "Look at all the fish you left." It's a little scary the way his big hands snap each tiny rib off the spine, the way he sucks them dry. There's something predatory about it, something that will not be denied. "Well," he says finally, "so here we are."

She jumps up, goes to the sink, begins to scrub at the frying pan with steel wool. Scrubs the pot, scrubs all the dishes, scrubs the sink and counter top, sweeps the floor. Finally, when she's asked him twice to lift his feet so she can sweep under them, he jams his cap back down onto his head and shoves the screen door open, and sits down heavily on the back porch. When she's done, when there's nothing left to clean or put away, and the front of her skirt is soaked with dishwater and her hair feels damp around her face, she goes outside. He's sitting on the edge of the porch, his arms draped over one of the horizontal two-by-fours that make up the framing for his greenhouse. It is so still and hot that even the cicadas sound subdued. "It's going to be beautiful," she says.

"What?"

"Your greenhouse." He raps one of the two-by-fours with his knuckles.

"One of these days," he says. He holds a hand up over his shoulder. "Let's see them."

"Stephen, you can't read anything in the dark."

"That's what *you* think," he says. But he comes in anyway, and rummages in a basket on top of the refrigerator while she rummages in her purse and when they converge again on the kitchen table she's smoothing out the long crisp onion-skin pages, and he's putting on his — glasses? She feels the same panic, exploding like light in front of her eyes, that she'd felt at the end of the driveway that day when he'd invoked the name of *need*. They give his face a drawn, pinched look like that of a man who has lived his life in a cold climate. He smooths down the sheets, begins to read, skimming down through the paragraphs, *whereas* after *whereas*, looking for the reason, following the lines with his finger so earnestly she can hardly stand to watch. She knows all the possibilities of his face. Anger, then sadness, then a wince, and he's there, he's made it — *irreconcilable differences*, it reads, this marriage is irretrievably broken.

The kitchen is too small and stuffy, too bright. It's her turn to go out and stand on the back porch and look at the pile of lumber, the roll of clear plastic, the framing that is Stephen's greenhouse-to-be. A morning-glory vine has climbed one of the posts and spread out over the roof, as though it couldn't wait, as though it wanted to come inside right now. The blooms, hundreds of them, are twisted shut and pointing toward the sky, but she knows they are blue, Heavenly Blues they're called. She saw them this afternoon, before they closed against the heat.

In the light coming from the kitchen door she sees writing on one of the two-by-fours, a penciled drawing of the greenhouse and its dimensions. She bends close to study it. Something's wrong here, she thinks. It's the two-by-fours, they're too widely spaced. They might not hold. Wouldn't you want to place them closer together so you could nail shelves to them on the inside? And that capped well on the other end of the porch, wouldn't you want to uncover it and see if it's still good? Wouldn't you want to extend the greenhouse around it, so you'd have water right there when you needed it? Wouldn't you want a higher ceiling so a person wouldn't have to stoop when she went inside? Wouldn't you want, Stephen, a place big enough for two people to work in, a place two people had a hand in, a kind of shelter? Quick, where's my pen? She slaps the pockets of her skirt.

When he's done, he takes off the glasses and lays them on the top page. "That just about covers it," he calls to her through the screen door. "That just about says it all." She's out there — he sees her — dangling her legs off the edge of the porch, leaning back on her hands with her hair un-

144

done and spread out across her shoulders. Then she turns. Through the open door, she sees him with his hands behind his head and his chair leaned against the wall, light striking the wings on his cap.

"Did you see where we both signed them?" she says. "Down there at the end. Did you see what we've done?"

Notes Toward an Understanding of My Father's Novel

THEY SAY that history repeats itself. My father is history and he certainly does. In his book about the Second World War he is young, he fights in the infantry in the Pacific, comes home and we are born. In this book, which is never finished, battle follows battle and they are links in the same chain leading home. In this book there is a river, the River Tor. It falls out of the New Guinea highlands and onto the jungle floor where it deepens and slows, gathering force for the spread through marshlands where the Tor floods into a many-branched delta of smaller rivers, all hurrying toward the bay. Where the Tor continuously becomes the bay, a wide fan of silt stains the water for miles, out beyond the last beaches and the headlands. My father detailed the shape and course and dividing line the Tor cut across the beach. He drew himself maps so he'd remember.

In his book, it's early 1942, New Guinea, daylight. There's a murk of heavy fog and beyond that fog, a beach that they must take. A metal ramp smacks the water. Men jump into the shallows, pointing their guns in all directions. They charge and crumple, dead and alive, onto the beach. One of these men is my father. The jungle explodes, flies at them. They cut their way in and the jungle turns quiet again, black and green, broken in half by the shells and bombs. What remains is someone's dream of the end of the world. My father stands up and looks at the wreckage and feels the breeze on his face, still hot from the fires, and finding himself alive, he examines himself slowly and with the patience of astonishment, to see what this might be that he has been allowed to keep. Back and forth an ambulance runs, a streak of green. In the middle of the night a blue flame wavers up under a coffeepot. It is the end of his thirty-fifth day in combat. The person shielding the flame, cupping his hands around it, is my father.

He wrote: "New Guinea, the night after the battle over the River Tor; I couldn't sleep so I got up and made a pot of coffee. I have something to tell my children: 'I was a second lieutenant,' I'll say, 'he's the one who stands up and says *Let's go, men.* I am the one who stood up and said that and came home alive. I tended the coffeepot all night long, seeing how small I could trim the flame underneath before it began to gutter. Everyone else was asleep all around me and I got the craziest idea that I was guarding them. You could watch their faces change; it must have been a trick of the light because some of them became boys and some of them grew old. I was the only one awake on the whole island of New Guinea, just me and the waves on the ocean and the night clouds flying by.'"

I know this story by heart. It's late 1946, he's been away for five years, longer than anyone he knows, but now he's home from the war and I'm born. Parades and celebrations. A few more years, then add my brother Simon. In the photographs from that time, my brother's weight confounds my father. Papa balances a frowning Simon, tipping him forward awkwardly so that the camera will record every line of the baby's body. My father's face is angular and handsome, a wide grin plumps up his cheeks, but above that smile his dark eyes hold you.

In one section of his book, time is measured by the miles he walked. Papa tries to be precise. He walked till he was lean, forced marches, forty, fifty miles a day, so many steps per mile, so many feet per step. He was in the infantry. *Infantry* is probably one of the first words I learned, and when I hear it now I hear the ring of cartridge belts, the knocking of canteens and the crunch of marching feet.

"We walked every island in the whole damn Pacific," he wrote. "I learned to sleep while we walked and the boy behind me held onto my pack so I wouldn't wander off and fall in a ditch somewhere. Now that's loyalty for you."

Many years later, the doctor who x-rayed my father's hips couldn't believe that anyone with such hip joints did not feel pain, but Papa insisted he did not. One of his hip joints was practically useless, locked in its socket, the other moved stiffly, like a jammed gear. The doctor couldn't understand: hip joints are the body's central pivots, so why no pain, no complaints all those years? He didn't know my father very well; his fear of weakness is as potent as the fear of ambush in enemy territory.

"Degenerative arthritis," the doctor said, "and you've had it for years."

"Nonsense," my father must have blustered, but when they showed him the x-rays, he could no longer argue the fact. But he'll argue the *cause* all night. My father insists that only he knows the real, the root cause of his condition:

the Second World War. He will listen to others, nodding in a distracted, amused way, but he still insists: his right hip deteriorated because for five years, when his bones were still forming, he marched and slept on the damp jungle ground of the Philippines, the Carolines and the island of New Guinea, in the Pacific, during the Second World War. He swears that the damp there penetrated his bones.

I went home for his birthday, in March of the year he found out about his condition. My mother called to say that he was feeling low. She said we'd all go down to Bristow's Island for the day and of course my brother Simon was coming too. When I got there the door flew open and down my father came, concentrating on each step. Papa is tall, loosely built, forceful; he still looks as though he carries something shiny coiled up inside. That year he carried himself carefully and he seemed to be listening to himself, inside himself, the way people do when they have a quarrel with their bodies. He was wearing a bright red tie decorated with tiny leaping tigers, and when he hugged me I smelled whiskey and soap and smoke in his shirt.

Later, as he showed his x-rays round the table, he said: "So I say 'You sure you got the right x-rays doctor, I don't feel as bad as those pictures look.' They didn't know what to make of me," he chuckled. We murmured and shook our heads.

"Look at all that calcified bone," he said, "I'm a tough old bird."

"Well, what are your options?" Simon asked. Simon is a lawyer. He thinks about all the angles.

"Oh, they make these stainless-steel hip joints now," Papa said, "I could have one of those put in, but I won't let them cut on me."

"There's always the wheelchair, tell them about that," my mother said. My father winked at us.

"She's more worried than I am," he said, "hell, I've lived with it this long."

Mother glared at him. "You're so strong," she said, "you don't know when something hurts you. And you won't know it until you wake up one day in a wheelchair with me pushing you around."

"Papa," I said, "don't you feel any pain really? You must."

His answer came, swift and fierce. "No," he said, defying us all, looking from one to the other warily as though *we* were the enemy and he our prisoner, standing firm, divulging nothing but name, rank, and serial number. At such times his face, always narrow and thoughtful, takes on a stubborn, beaked look. "It's stiffness mostly," he said. "It comes and goes. It's something I have to live with, so let's not make a federal case out of it. I limped almost as soon as I got back from the war. Something like that ages you, that's all."

His book begins in the living room of his parent's house on the day the Japanese bombed Pearl Harbor, an ordinary enough place to begin. They have assembled a foursome for bridge – my father and his wife of five months, his father and mother. The radio plays low in the background. I imagine the shadows of oak limbs on the wide pine floorboards, a dance of sunlight and shade, and the dry pine branches piled in the fireplace crackling as the flames seized them, filling the room with the clean smell of pitch that nobody noticed because it was the smell of any winter day. Then the announcement, the day of infamy, and my father is training in a red clay field in Georgia that has been scraped bare, then trampled hard by the marching. Then he is rocking on the ocean for weeks, months, in a troopship with only the horizon in sight, becalmed, sometimes, for days.

"I feel everyone I care for is with me now," he wrote. "They're here and they comfort me."

One day, his father's death overtakes my father. The news arrives in a packet of letters. He's aboard ship, there's no chance he can go home on leave.

"Many emotions," he wrote. "I felt many emotions."

I used to flip forward through the pages beyond his father's death, looking for something more, but I knew I wouldn't find it. His father's death, where would it lead him who was already so far from home? Into the wilds of grief? The jungles that are so rank the path grows over behind you even as you walk? Best to stand firm, to insist. The way Papa tells it, his father's death happened to someone else. Each time I read those words, *many emotions*, I'm aware of a dead spot inside, no bigger than a thumb, but cold. I have no words for his grief, I have only his words to us, and though they seldom spoke directly of grief, they were full of grief inside.

Our town was home to many of these men, Papa's friends, survivors of the Bataan Death March, survivors of the Air Force or the infantry. They greeted each other on the streets with clasped handshakes. They marched together on Veterans Day; their faces slid by, eyes fixed beyond the crowd. It was after one such parade that I left home for the final time.

I had made a mistake, a miscalculation of loyalty, and

had come home after college to teach in the local high school. I was dying there. I don't regret that it happened, I only wish it had gone by faster and cleaner than it did. On the day of the parade that year, three of us, who called ourselves refugees, climbed into the second story of a deserted building on Main Street and unfurled from the window the biggest, rattiest American flag we could find. For every star, there was a matching hole. But every one of the vets who looked up saluted grimly — what else could they do to a flag? — as we cheered and waved the flag and showered them with soap bubbles.

"What have I raised?" my father demanded to know when he caught up with me after the parade. "Tell me, what in hell have I raised?" He was wearing his khaki uniform; silver bars gleamed on his cap, the Purple Heart on his chest, the lieutenant's chevron on the sleeve.

"Your daughter," I said. "Me. Annie."

"My daughter doesn't mock me," he said. His eyes were red-rimmed, hard.

"I'm not mocking you."

He pointed to the flag draped over my arm. "Then what the hell were you doing?"

"Papa," I said, but he wheeled and hurried off down the street. I cannot speak for my father but I know what I saw that day — I saw a man who had been betrayed, for whom betrayal was like death, whom I had killed this time, I had cut a thread — call this one loyalty — that holds the world together.

We sang: *Happy birthday dear Papa, haaaapy birthday to you.* My mother and Simon and I put our heads together in imitation of a barbershop quartet and we sang the harmonies we'd practiced. We sang them three times, until Papa got impatient and blew out the candles. There were eight circles of eight candles, which meant he was sixty-four that year, and he made some joke about the cake getting too crowded and how he'd have to stay thirty-nine for a while longer. He's been thirty-nine for close to twenty-five years. He says he's waiting for us to catch up with him. My father has visions: hard times come, another Great Depression, and all of us are forced to live together again, eking out a living from our little piece of ground, getting by, just the four of us. He says that we will all be together again. Being *from* someplace is important, he says, because it means you can never be lost. There are things you carry inside you, like seeds, he says, planted before you were born, that pull you back to that place where you belong, to the people who love you, that will carry you through nights when only you know where you are: crouched in a foxhole listening for the sound of a human footstep.

For his birthday that year, my father got a book of Matthew Brady's Civil War photographs from Simon, a new pair of tennis shoes and a flock of azalea bushes from Mother, and, from me, an album by the Sons of the Pioneers. He loves this music, cowboy music, all twangy with steel guitars and voices that wail lonesome out under a high desert sky. In particular, he loves one cut by the Sons of the Pioneers, the song "Cool Water," which is all about mirages in the desert and men who don't succumb to their fatal spell, men who keep moving. He moved the needle back, played it through again: *"Take a listen, Dan,"* they sang, *"Don't you listen to him, man / He's a devil not a man /*

And he spreads the burning sand with water." "Water,"
someone sings in the background, the voice of the mirage
calling. He sat there listening, a glass of bourbon resting on
his knee, the lamp casting his face into stony angles. When
the lines came around he nodded along, as though he had
just heard a wise man speak.

When I leaned over that night and kissed my father
goodnight, he was sleeping; he brushed his hand across his
cheek as though a moth had grazed him. At night, the
house creaks and settles and grows so still I swear I can
hear us all breathing from our separate rooms, forming for
that moment the unbroken circle our lives will never make.
Back in the pine woods a whippoorwill sang; in the distance, a siren sounded its alarm. And I thought about how
Papa had talked that afternoon, how it had been part of
the same story he is always trying to tell.

That afternoon, relaxed and in a generous mood, he
wanted to give us something. He went back to a war to
find it, this time to the Battle of Gettysburg, the fight for
the Round Tops. He spoke as if it had happened yesterday
or to someone he knew. Ask him, he knows how many
men were deployed at Little Round Top, he knows the
order of the regiments that formed Pickett's last long line.
He knows why Lee ordered them forward up the slope and
straight into the guns, wave after wave. Ask him, he will
tell you about courage, he will tell you, with urgency in his
voice, on page after page of scratched-over lines, how many
survived the landing at Luzon. Ask him, he will go on until
he gets it right, until he says it clear enough for anyone to
hear. But what is he trying to say?

I remembered the time years before at Gettysburg, when

Simon and I were children. We had driven to Pennsylvania via Harper's Ferry, Manassas, Antietam, our living history lesson for that summer. My father leaned on the fence surrounding the copse of trees that is the northern boundary of Pickett's charge, the high-water mark of the Confederacy. He loves those words — *high-water mark*. To this day they roll from him clear and sad.

Who was I then?

Eldest, namer of battlefields, bearer of kerosene lanterns, reader of battlefield maps, my father's daughter.

At night beside our fire he dramatized the battle day by day. He added characters and gave us parts to play. "There's a courier out there somewhere tonight," he said; his hand swept across the stars that stretched from horizon to horizon. "He's carrying a message from General Lee to General Heth. Where's this courier from, do you suppose?"

"Georgia?" Simon and I said in one small voice.

"What's he got to tell General Heth?"

" 'Close up the flank, General,' " Simon volunteered, " 'we can't leave a weak spot in the line.' "

"And does he get through, this courier from Georgia?" Papa leaned over us, waiting. "No," he prompted, and the three of us said it: "No."

Daylight, next day, the third day's field at Gettysburg, the edge of the woods along Seminary Ridge where the Confederate lines formed for Pickett's charge. We stood in the shadow of the North Carolina monument, a broken wheel of men straining forward, hands shading their eyes as they study the field they must cross, every line in every face pulled tight.

"Close your eyes," my father said. He would read to us from the diary of a Union soldier who saw them charge. I shook my head no, afraid to slip into that dark. "No, I don't have to." I shook my head till I was dizzy, trying to drown out the sound of his voice. He read and I looked at the wheat field; the heat above the young yellow grain rose and danced in the air. He read: " 'We saw an overwhelming resistless tide of an ocean of armed men sweeping upon us. On they move as with one soul, in perfect order over ridge and slope, through orchard and meadow and cornfield, magnificent, grim, irresistible.' "

My father has his prejudices. He jokes that he's never been wrong, but I believe he means it, because when he is wrong he always seems startled. I think of all the times at breakfast, lunch, or dinner, of the knives and forks slapped down, of the silences, then the rising sounds of argument, while he denounced this, embraced that. We never argue about anything that matters to us, but we do argue for a reason. We argue politics so that we may raise our voices and so that, in the excitement of the moment, we may draw close. Sometimes I believe I could come back anytime and step right into the same disagreements, altered slightly to fit the year.

Papa started it the morning of his birthday. "It seems to me," he said, "that we've got to have congressmen who are accountable." His forefinger hit the table precisely on *accountable* and thumped out the rest of the sentence. "We should be able to call them *back* from Washington and say what the *hell* have you been *doing* there spending *our* money."

"No," I said, "what we need is a new way of doing things, we don't need to slow down a system that's already a dinosaur."

"No," said Simon, "what we need is a system with built-in provisions for swift recall votes."

"Well if it wasn't for all those damn give-away programs we wouldn't have problems anyway," said my mother, who cuts through to first causes.

Simon's argument lacked its usual legal elegance. Sometimes, when he speaks, Simon draws arabesques of reason in the air. When he lifted his coffee cup, his hand shook. Then Simon said: "I have to go back to Atlanta early, tomorrow. I have a big case on Tuesday and I have to get ready for it, I won't be able to go to Bristow's with you all, I'm sorry."

Papa didn't comment, he didn't even look at Simon or change expression. He wiped his mouth, got up from the table, and walked out.

"Now what's eating him?" Simon asked through clenched teeth.

"You know," I said, "anytime one of us is leaving he gets like this."

Simon looked trapped. "Christ," he said, throwing down his napkin, "everything's fine until you cross him, then *bang*, it's like you didn't exist anymore."

"He's been like that for years, you know he's not going to change," Mother said. "He cannot stand to let you go any sooner than he has to, you know that."

"Yeah, is that so?" said Simon, and his lip curled just like it used to when we were small and he was cornered. "He has a wonderful way of showing it."

"Simon's right and you know it," I said to my mother.

"Why bother?" he said, "I mean, a person has to ask himself that question some damn time."

"*Simon,*" my mother snapped. I laughed but I stopped, because I thought that he might break something or collapse on the table at last in a grand show of frustration and defeat, the first to happen in our family since the Civil War. But no. Simon is my father's son as surely as I am my father's daughter: a show of temper would leave him open to attack. He ducked his head and pushed back from the table and walked outside without a word, slamming the door behind him.

After a minute or two I followed Simon, leaving Mother there angrily clearing dishes from the table. I stepped out into the back yard in time to watch Simon march off down the street. I heard Papa banging around in the tool shed. Soon he came out with hammer and a coffee can full of nails and started in on the back fence. He hammers the way he marches in Veterans Day parades, the way he lives — with his back held straight and a job to do. Each blow landed true, and the whole fence shuddered. He hammered as though he'd been given only so much time to strengthen this fence against what was coming to knock it down.

Sometimes I think that in Papa the war is an old river, patiently working its way through rocky land, finding new channels when old ones are blocked. That it comes on, magnificent, grim, irresistible as the sight of Pickett's men making their charge, wave after wave, tide after tide, so many thrown against so many guns that the miracle is that anyone survives. But what is carried forward on that tide? What would he have us remember? This is as much as I can say — my father loves lost causes, ordeals, the great fighters, people who cling to the sides of mountains, rope gone, fingers loosening. He loves the hopeless cases, people who wrestle with God and go down, looking Him straight in the eye. I know that he loves both victory and defeat since both must be met with strength and courage. And I know that if he could, he would give us the great thing that he knows — how he came home alive.

These were the trappings, the things of which our childhood was made:

The Samurai sword, made of steel so pure it is silver-white. "Toward the end of the war, they charged against us with these, can you imagine? They were desperate," he said. "They charged against our machine guns with *these*. The emperor ordered them to do it and they did. Fools," he said, carving at the air with the sword, and there was sadness and wonder too in that word as if he cared more for their crazy, doomed courage than he cared that they were The Enemy. "They were the cream of the crop," he said, "the bravest and strongest. And when we saw their eyes just before they charged, we thought every time they might make it."

I have seen their eyes.

The fear: of weakness, the crippler, the disease of weakness. So that when one muffled winter morning, we all lost an infant daughter, a sister on whose mouth the stern set of my father's mouth already lay, he turned away and would let no one see his eyes and we saw instead that there was something shameful in loss and grief, something weak that no one must see.

The reasons: We stood outside a Chinese restaurant in a tight-faced, low-voiced huddle. My father refused to go in.

"Oh it's Chinese for God's sake, not Japanese," Mother said.

"I don't know," he answered, musing up into the sky, "yellow skin makes my trigger finger itchy. I have my principles."

But I was angrier than them all. I pushed between Simon and Mother to stand there face-to-face with him and I said: "Papa, that was twenty years ago."

He looked at me in mock surprise: "I'll tell you what," he said, "time has nothing to do with it." And I saw him swept backwards – the current is strong – until he met his younger self, the soldier, and came to rest.

So then if time has nothing to do with it, we come close to the present moment: my father and I, squared off across the dining-room table, speaking in low vehement voices about Hiroshima, Nagasaki, and Vietnam. I am speaking to him as though he'd set them in motion. I am speaking of the sins of the fathers, of the steel of those blades and bayonets, the blue steel gun barrels, of how the hard boots and helmets, the bombs that saved them have returned, bringing death to their children. Simon was spared, I say, but only because he is too young.

"Annie," he says, "how can I make you understand? We were going in," he says, he's pleading. "We had our equipment. We were going to invade Japan." His hands grip the edge of the table. "They estimated we would have sustained eighty-five percent casualties. You might not even be here if it hadn't been for that bomb."

I get up from the table and leave the room, leave the

thought of that explosion. But I see it behind me, the cloud rising over Hiroshima, his life and my life joined in that flash of light. My life comes out of that fire.

Peace. After the Japanese surrender, my father went to those northern beaches where he would have fought had the bomb not ended the war. He walked the narrow strip of beach between the gun implacements and the ocean out of which they would have risen and fought. There, I lose him. His book stops here and I cannot imagine what he felt, only that it was dark and strong, this feeling of being alive, delivered, spared.

In our family, it's customary that on our birthdays we wear or assemble or plant what we've been given. Nobody remembers how this began, but it's a ritual. Toward sunset on that birthday I went out into the back yard and found Papa there digging holes for the azaleas Mother had given him. The yard is choked with flowering shrubs. He wore his new tennis shoes and he dug back along the fence line. He aimed each jab of the shovel. In the fading watery sunlight the skin on his forehead looked thin, the bone was a fact underneath, and seeing this I was suddenly afraid. Every time I looked, that bone jumped out as though there were a light behind it. I don't know if he noticed my staring, but he looked up and said: "I'm worried about your mother."

"Why," I asked, "what's wrong with her?"

"Too many cigarettes," he said, "and too many drinks before dinner."

"Have you said anything to her?"

"In my own way," he said. "I told her 'Why don't you stop drinking for a week, just to see how you feel.' She just looked at me with that resentful look she gets, so I shut up. I don't know, you can't help."

Before I could stop to be sad for their silences, my father was off again. He was reminded of his sister who was having a lot of trouble with one of her kids. It seemed that nothing could be done. Soon we were gossiping about each of his brothers and sisters in turn. My father loves to gossip and so do I. We sorted through reasons, probed for meaning in each person's dilemma. In the end, we found a clue, a flaw or an error that seemed to lie at the root of the trouble. "Now what do you make of that?" he said. And I said what I made of it and, satisfied, he could go on. My father's shovel flashed and turned and then it slowed, and stopped. He leaned on the handle catching his breath, his weight resting on his good leg, staring into the woods beyond the backyard fence. The wind was blowing toward us, blowing his pant legs flat against him, and I noticed that one leg was thinner than the other and my heart hammered. I might as well have come across him naked, and I looked away. He was still staring, leaning on the shovel, paying no attention to me.

"I'm trying to think," he said, "which birthday it was that I spent in New Guinea."

"Which one?" I said.

He seemed not to have heard. He chipped at the ground with the shovel. "It was the River Tor, so I must have been twenty-two that year. Have I told you this before?"

I shook my head no. I'd read it in his book where it exists in several forms and styles and places, inserted here and there like a polestar around which the whole constellation wheels, but I had never heard him tell it.

"We had to cross a branch of the Tor to get to the battle, and they were bringing the dead and the wounded back across just upriver from us. They had dumped the dead ones all along the banks because they needed stretchers and there was this one boy, they laid him out there right where I was about to cross. I thought I knew him; he looked like someone from back home, so I went closer but then I saw that I'd never seen him before and that was worse. I felt like a spy, but I couldn't look away. He'd been shot in the stomach and his guts were crawling out so slow they didn't look like they were moving, but they were piling up on the sand beside him. I wanted to scoop them up and put them back but I couldn't move. I just kept standing there thinking to myself 'That man's *life* is leaving him right here in front of my eyes.'" He shook himself and started digging; he jabbed the blade deep and left it there. "And then, I did the damndest thing. They tell me this battle fatigue was a pretty common thing and that must have been what came over me because I squatted down there and I kept my hand on the boy's shoulder until he was gone. I remember thinking 'Goddammit, he shouldn't die like this.' And you know, I *knew* when he was gone," he said. He held up his hand and stared at the palm. "I didn't have to see anything to let me know, just all of a sudden there was nothing under my hand any longer and that's when I realized there had been *something* there before. And that's when I broke and ran like hell. Isn't that the damndest thing you've ever heard? Well," he said, as he threw a clod of dirt out of the hole he was digging, "now you know your father has his weak side."

"Weak?" I said. "You call that weak?"

"Yes, weak, that's what I said. Why do you question everything I say?" And he went back to his digging.

I walked toward the house and when I got there my heart was roaring in my ears. I grabbed a sweater and walked away into the woods behind the house. The tops of the pines were gleaming in the sun's last light. I walked up one hill, then down the other side, and the country looked strange to me, though I'd been there many times before. I know it would feel good to run, so I ran as fast as I could and that didn't feel good enough. So I ran faster while the sand tried to hold me back. I ran till I felt a pain in my side, then I slid down onto the pine needles, palms and knees skidding, and rested, and when I got up I thought it would feel good to shout, to hear the sound of my voice, so I shouted and even that was not enough, so I ran some more. I thought I could run beyond the fear that pushed me to run, but it was still there and I had run as fast as I could run. So I sat on the ground for a long time and thought about my father and the man he had believed he knew. I kept thinking of his hand, how it had rested there on the man's shoulder, a link in a circle that joined his own spared life to the finished life of the other, and how, brought into that circle, he must have felt his own life come onto him, real as fire, real as water, as certain to disappear. And how he carried that knowledge with him into the next battle and the next, then home to his family, to Simon and Mother and to me where I sat under the wind that sounded like water as it rushed in among the tops of the pines.

Early in the morning my father said goodbye to Simon, standing in the driveway beside my brother's idling car.

Both their faces were blank as they shook hands. I ran up and hugged Simon, I squeezed him until he said "Hey" nervously and shook himself loose. Then my mother hugged him and then he was gone, trailing exhaust. My father smacked his forehead: "I meant to tell him to get that tail-pipe fixed, it's dangerous; it worries me that he'd take his children for a ride in a car with a faulty tailpipe," he said. He looked down the road as though he could call Simon back, and his face looked old and tired.

But by the time we had the car loaded down with crab nets and fishing poles, all the paraphernalia for a trip to the island, he was cheerful again and in command. As he slid behind the wheel, he winced, he grabbed his bad leg in both hands and hoisted it into the car and he swore under his breath. But when he saw me watching, he grinned and pointed to his leg: "Stiffness," he said. And by the time we were thirty miles from town, he was laughing and joking and singing with my mother, some old Cole Porter duet that had come to their minds as they'd passed a certain spot in the road.

The closer we came to the coast, the more a balance tipped – the human shrank before the rising of the wild. Down below Barnwell, houses began to look frail and brittle as the nests of dirt-daubers. The broad black fields were miles long, miles deep, turned over for spring planting. The first water oaks appeared beside the road, hung with Spanish moss. The piny woods became so thick and tangled with undergrowth the sun didn't shine there: it intruded.

Beyond the last town, the tidal creeks and solitary shacks began. Before we reached this town, we saw smoke that rose and hung low in stone-shaped clouds over the line of trees. As we approached, the smoke turned oily, dark black, and around one curve we came on a shack that was burning in tall, sharp flames. The fire was out of control and people milled around in the yard in an aimless sort of way. The fire seemed to flow and whirl around the house, billowing out of windows, bursting free from under the eaves. We slowed to pass through the line of cars parked on either shoulder and a woman ran out in front of the car and tried to motion us over to the side of the road. She ran with jerky motions, flapping her hands. Her eyes looked at nothing. "This must be her house," I said, and my father looked over his shoulder and frowned. "Not much left to own," he said.

She was a thin, weevil-faced white woman in a faded dress and bedroom slippers. She kept her arms folded over her chest, holding herself as if she were cold. As she came close to the car, my father's hand snuck up the door panel and pressed the lock. I felt ashamed for him. But fear is contagious and the longer she looked into the car, the more I saw what had scared him: she looked familiar, though where I'd seen her before I couldn't say. She peered in at us, craning her neck, looking for something, her eyes gray and vacant.

"That poor woman," my mother said, "now she has to start all over. I can't imagine how awful that would be," she said.

"People should take better care," my father said in an irritated voice. Waving the woman away, he gunned the car back out onto the open road. "Somebody was probably careless, or drunk," he said, in the judgmental voice used by fathers who have come through destruction and who think they know its face. He had seen that face, and now was he saying that by staying small and neat, by keeping low and doing the right thing, you could save yourself? As we drove away, I thought of that woman, blind in her grief, asking for help from all who passed by. I knew her and my father knew her too, that's why he locked the door.

Nobody spoke while we crossed the causeway, a narrow neck of green stretched across the marsh. The deeper you go into the low country, the more fertile the land becomes. On the island, the long laps and undulations of black ground couldn't have been plowed much longer than a week, yet the furrows were already fuzzy with green and the trees were luminous with a pale green light. The strength of this country, the low country, is that it is always forming. I count on that country, on that strength, that forming and dying and forming again. In my heart I return there daily. It is a place where nothing is ever the same, where the past is soon overtaken by new green shoots and vines.

Coming to Bristow's Island I can almost believe that we have made it once again back to the beginning of the world where everything carries on a life that seems eternal. Snowy egrets pace the shallows of a maze of tidal creeks; on the open beach sponges by the hundreds, jellyfish, sand dollars, and mats of strong-smelling seaweed are flung by one tide, reclaimed by the next. A steady traffic of brown pelicans flies low, in squadrons, to and from the rookery at the end of the island. But of course it's not the beginning of the world. There are dangers here, any one of them could close a person's life. There are the gray rock jetties covered with oyster shells and barnacles sharp as razors and the channels cut by the tide, which look shallow until you look deeper and see, below the surface, an undertow, like darkness going by at an incredible pace. Nevertheless, for the hell of it and because the sky was blue and full of tall thunderheads, that day I climbed out onto one of the jetties to see if my balance had kept pace with my nerve. I sucked in my breath and balanced as I have done so many times it has become second nature. And for a moment, same as always, with my arms outstretched, I heard my heart beating like a warning, heard something rejoicing to find itself alive on that rock with the sharp shells below, the ocean beyond.

While my father fished from the end of another rock jetty, I worked the crab net for my mother. She can catch crabs where there are none. She is strong and clever and sly then. She played them slowly, winding up the string, pulling in the greedy crab that clung to the rotten meat. And when the crab was visible in the shallow water, I pounced and scooped it into the net. We worked together that way. By midday we had filled a bushel basket with crabs but my father hadn't caught one fish. The sun hung overhead in a hazy sky and the top of my father's head was turning red. It was low tide and the flat silver water washed listlessly at the base of the rocks. He stood up straight and kept casting and reeling, casting and reeling. My mother and I wandered down to the rocks and called to him. "Aren't you getting too hot out there?" my mother called. "Let's eat," she said. But he waved us aside. We ambled up into the shade of the fringe of palmetto trees back of the beach. We spread the picnic cloth and waited. He kept fishing. I went to call my father.

He didn't hear me when I called from the end of the rocks. He was within the sound of the breakers. So I climbed out onto the rocks. Weaving lightly, with an eye on the barnacles, I reached him and tapped him on the shoulder. He started, then turned, wincing. I saw fear spread into his eyes. His leg was twisted at an odd angle and he gritted his teeth and gave his leg an angry shove with one hand.

"What?" he said. "What is it?"

"Come eat," I said. "It's ready, we're hungry."

"Go ahead," he said. "You two go ahead. I'm staying right here until I catch one," he said, pointing to the rock below his feet.

For once I did not raise my voice in argument. What was there to argue? That he couldn't catch a fish, that he was in pain, and afraid? Beyond the jetty a fish jumped; it flashed silver, then plopped back into the water and disappeared, leaving a ring of brine to mark the spot. "Look there," I said, and I touched his shoulder. "Big one."

He had already hauled back the rod. "Got it," he said. He cast as if he were throwing a javelin at a target, his lips pressed tight. "Come here, dammit," he said.

I threaded my way back off the rocks and went to sit with Mother in the thin shade up under the palmettos. I think of my father now and I think this: he stands on the rock and I wander on the beach and this distance roars between us, a river heard from far away. Most of the time, though we are crossing that river, we do not cross. But crossing is all we know.

All Set About
with Fever Trees

IN MACON, Georgia, my grandmother, Mariah Palmer, was a famous teacher. She took up this career after her husband died during the Depression, leaving her with three small children to look after. From that time on, she taught English in the Bibb County schools and Sunday school at the First Presbyterian Church. Later, when the wine of her understanding had clarified and aged to her satisfaction, she taught the Bible at the YWCA, where all seats were filled, so I've heard, when her topic was the Book of John, that great gospel of abiding faith. Then, at sixty, she announced to us all that she'd signed on to teach the children of the Presbyterian missionaries in the Belgian Congo in Africa.

For days after she got the news, my mother went around worrying out loud to herself. Folding the laundry, she'd snap a towel and say "Well, damn," as if she were determined to have her say, even if she'd already lost the argument. I overheard them talking once when my grandmother came to visit that summer before she left for Africa. They were sitting out on the screened porch, stringing and snapping beans for supper. My mother is a master at subtle persuasion. Not for her the direct attack. She prefers to sketch an outline of danger and leave you to fill in the rest. Driving by a black juke-joint called the Royal Peacock Club, for instance, she had recently taken to slowing down and pointing out to me the slash marks in the black vinyl door, and the men, with hats cocked low over their eyes, who were bothering women and shoving each other around outside, and though I was only eight years old, I knew that this was a piece of some puzzle that I was supposed to hold onto until I was old enough to realize where it fit and what I was being warned against.

That particular day, Mother selected her somber colors – muddy browns and greens – and with these she painted pictures for my grandmother of the lonely life she would lead over in Africa. Then she selected the darker earth-tones and with these she made her picture of an aging, ailing body, of brittle bones, a failing mind, all set against the black background of death itself. When this was over she sighed: "I've had my say, not that it makes any difference."

"Good," my grandmother said. "It's always better to get these things off your chest than to keep them bottled up inside. But I will tell you, my best beloved," she said, "I have done a lot of praying in my short and happy life and I can now report to you with confidence that I have never been surer of anything. As it happens, I have heard the clear call down deep in my soul and it is summoning me to labor in the fields far from the fleshpots of civilization."

This was good stuff. I stood there hugging myself, feeling the goosebumps run along my arms as I imagined how her eyes must look – like Moses' eyes in her illustrated copy of the Old Testament – two points of leaden fire aimed at the idolaters as they danced around their golden calf: fleshy women and men with small pointed beards playing tambourines and writhing around together. "Fleshpots," I said to myself, and I remembered the way the fire blazed up in the trash barrel outside the door of the Royal Peacock Club on cold winter nights, throwing shadows on the black faces, and the way the whiskey bottles flashed in that light. And I wanted her to go to Africa and stay as long as she wished, as long as it took to find whatever had called her. I wanted her to go because lately I had had glimmerings in myself, intimations of some kind of destiny that was waiting for me, somewhere, with my name, Annie Vess, already written on it in big bright letters. Sometimes when I was sitting in the library at school or running on the playground or even at supper with my family, everything would get very quiet inside me and then a glowing would begin, followed by a burst of light, like a bomb going off up in the air, and I would feel that something was about to speak, to show me the way I was meant to go.

While she was gone, I kept a map of Africa thumbtacked to the wall of my room and circled her town, Lubondai, and every other place she mentioned, in red. Her letters arrived covered with stamps that featured regal black heads held high on thin necks, a white queen in her jewels, a king who looked like a walrus with his mustache and his heavy staring expression. The paper smelled sweet and dusty, the way Africa must smell, I thought, sun-warmed and lush, like hay. I imagined her writing these letters, alone there in the middle of the continent, in a hut late at night, with the lantern burning beside her. I saved them and studied them by flashlight under the covers before I fell asleep, speed-reading through the parts about how their houses were nice houses just like those back in the States, with plumbing and curtains and all, and about the well-mannered Christian children she was fortunate to be teaching, and hurrying on to the paragraphs that described her travels.

She wrote that she traveled by Land Rover, along roads where the vines grew so fast the driver had to get out now and then and hack the road clear. In the snapshot she sent along with one letter, the driver is naked to the waist and black as carved onyx, while she is as serene as the Queen Mother, her broad-brimmed straw hat lying on her lap. "On the road to Lulluraburg," the caption read, "to hear a chorus of native voices sing Bach, Handel, and Brahms." "A fifty-thousand-acre game preserve," read another caption enclosed with a postcard that was divided into four sections and showed elephants, giraffes, lions, and antelopes. "The Mountains of the Moon," she wrote. "Imagine, Annie, mountains nineteen thousand feet high, so high that even viewed up-close, they look far away." Sometimes I would dream of these places, the Mountains of the Moon and a chorus of golden lions singing as they galloped up and down the slopes.

When I showed my mother one of these letters or a postcard, she would shake her head, sigh, and say, "It certainly sounds like Mother's found what she's been looking for."

"Which is?"

She would shrug, roll her eyes. "Beats me."

I kept the faith, waiting for the day when my grandmother would come back and tell me everything she knew about clear calls and destiny. I was patient in my waiting because I believed in her. She knew things. She would not fail. She had powers that other people did not have. There is, for instance, a memory, not a dream, that I have of her, and of myself as a child in her house in Macon, which will show you what I mean. In this memory, I've gone downstairs by myself at night, looking for a drink of water. The light from the streetlights comes through the tall windows and makes shapes like tall lighted doors across the floors. So I start for one and find myself standing in the corner of a room, start for another and end up facing the wall. I've not made a sound but my grandmother comes down from upstairs, tying her bathrobe as she comes, flipping light switches until we reach the kitchen, and when she flips that switch, everything is white — the enamel of the table top, the kitchen sink, the bowl of paper-white narcissus just coming into bloom, her bathrobe and the ruff of white hair standing out around her head, the glass of milk she sets in front of me.

And then she lifts me and holds me so close to her face I can see the flecks of gold in her bright hazel eyes and the tiny roses etched along the gold rims of her thick glasses, and she sets me down on her lap. From the shelf above the kitchen table, from beside the bowl of narcissus, she has taken down a book, the *Just So Stories* by Rudyard Kipling, and slowly, surely, as I listen to her heartbeat and the sound of her voice humming against my back, the bewildered way I had felt as I wandered from room to room, like a small leaf floating in a cold sea of light, leaves me. And we are gone into that country on the banks of the great, gray, green, greasy Limpopo River, all set about with fever trees, where life first stirred and crawled from the mud. Where the rhino got his baggy skin, the whale his throat, the leopard his spots, where the cat walked by himself waving his wild

wild tail, and the humans made the first letter and then the entire alphabet. Where everything is about first causes, sources, what stirs within the seed that causes the plant to grow. " 'Hear and attend and listen,' " she reads, " 'for this befell and behappened and became, O My Best Beloved, when the Tame animals were wild.' "

As she reads and reads I drowse and float close to sleep, feel the house all around us, sleeping and dark, except for this room. And then I'm growing, I'm rising out through the roof and flying over the planet, searching until I find Macon, Georgia, on the banks of the Ocmulgee River, sleeping in its grove of dark pines, and in the middle of that city I find the room where we are reading, set against the dark like the North Star. And below the windy ocean of darkness that runs around the world, that lighted room remains.

The summer I was twelve, my grandmother came back to the States and we went to Macon to welcome her home. I had prepared for days with a notebook full of questions to ask her. What was it in your experience which most clearly answered the call that took you there? What unusual or exciting experiences did you have that give us a clue to the differences between people? Did anything happen to you there that has convinced you of anything or shaken any previously held beliefs?

Macon, Georgia, straggles along the banks of the great grave Ocmulgee River, which is a broad, slow river, sluggish as its name. In the summer, the sky is always white, as though a layer of smoke hangs between you and everything you want to see, and the sun burns behind this haze like a white metal disk. "The only difference between Macon, Georgia, and hell," my father said, as we drove across the bridge and into the city, "is that a river runs through Macon."

"A river runs through hell, too," I said, "if what you mean by hell is the underworld. It's called the River Styx." I knew because I had just finished reading a book called *Great Myths of the Western World* and added it to the list on my summer reading-club card at the public library.

"Then I guess there's no difference at all," he said.

In the same church basement where we'd told her good-bye four years earlier, we spread the long tables with yellow tablecloths and set out platters of chicken and potato salad, green beans, and a thickly iced cake shaped like Africa with the Belgian Congo outlined in red and with a small green flag stuck in the center to show where she'd lived. I was the one responsible for the flag.

As I helped to set the tables, I kept one eye on the doorway and the excitement turned inside me like a bright whirligig going round and round. As I slid down the halls and in and out of the Sunday school rooms with my pack of cousins, I kept an ear tuned to the noise in the other room. To this day, I don't know exactly what I'd hoped to see, but when she walked through the door, something died in me with the sudden fading sound that a record makes when the plug is pulled on the machine. It was my grandmother, arms open wide to welcome everyone, and was she fat! She must have gained thirty pounds, and she looked like a flour sack tied in the middle, with her black patent-leather belt cinched tight around the waist of her gaudy blue-and-pink print dress.

I remember I tried to escape but it was too late. She wrapped me in her flabby arms and pulled me into her bosom where I thought I might suffocate on the smell of English Lavender cologne and Vicks Vapo-Rub. She rocked me, weeping, calling me her best beloved, the heart of her heart, the light of her life. And then I was weeping too, the whole place was weeping. She would take off her glasses, wipe her eyes, look at me, and we'd both burst into tears again. But I wasn't weeping for the joy of seeing her again. I was weeping because I'd been betrayed. Because she'd crossed the equator and received a scroll signed by Neptune, ruler of the deep. Because she'd sailed up the Congo River as far as it might be sailed. Because she'd climbed halfway up the great Pyramid of Cheops at Giza, she'd visited the Sphinx and heard the riddle. She'd even walked the streets of Paris, France, on her way back home. Because she'd done all those things and then she'd come back fat. That was the only change, much less miracle, that had happened to her.

Now all she could do was argue and eat, eat and argue. She tore the paper tablecloth with her pen, drawing maps and lines and arrows. This tribe, that tribe. What does the Mau-Mau uprising have to do with the one clear call? That's what I wanted to know. Meanwhile, she ate four wedges of cornbread soaked with butter, three pieces of chicken, and a biscuit. She ate fresh peach cobbler topped with two scoops of ice cream. She ate after everyone else had laid down their forks. My mother said, "My God, Mother, how could you let yourself gain all that weight?"

"Daughter mine," she said. "I did not plan it that way. I became fond of the native diet, which consists mostly of starch, and, well, these things happen in this great world of ours."

"What do they eat?" I asked, shoving the last of my banana pudding into the potato salad.

"A root called *manioc*, my best beloved," she said, fishing for another slab of cornbread. "It's like our sweet potato. They dry this manioc root and pound it into flour and they make a bread with the flour that's called *bidia*. They dunk this bread" – she dunked the cornbread into the gravy boat and held it up, dripping – "in palm-oil gravy, and they call it food for the hunter inside."

"That's gross," I said. She laughed and I saw all the gold fillings in her teeth. Later, as we watched slides of Africa that consisted mostly of a dozen different views of a row of mustard-colored concrete-block houses, with here and there a view of the Mountains of the Moon seen through a herd of curious giraffes, I hashed over the story about the roots. There in the land of the one clear call, in the shadow of the Mountains of the Moon, they scratched in the dirt and ate roots. From that point on, I could not have cared less about anything. I imagined that I was sitting up on a high bald rock, too high even for eagles to reach, looking down on everyone as they crowded close to see the treasures she'd collected – the broad-bladed knives etched with intricate woven patterns, the hammered-copper crosses, the raffia baskets and carved wooden bowls and ivory crosses, the shaman's headpiece that was covered in leopard skin and had cold eyes, a fiercely sucking mouth, and perfect little ears made of clay. I watched as she lined up a troop of ivory elephants in order of descending size. The smallest was no larger than the nail of your smallest finger, and each was carved in perfect detail, from the flapping ears down to the moon-shaped toes. I watched as she modeled the latest fashion from the Congo — a braided straw rope with two tassles of coarse black hair attached, to be worn around the waist like a skirt.

I watched it all from my bald rock high above the valley. But when she came to my gift I would gladly have died. I was her favorite, so they said, and when she called me to the front of the room everyone turned their tender smiling silence, their tearful happiness, my way. I unwrapped the tissue paper she'd pressed into my hand, and there in my palm was a wooden pin — a brown, antelope-like creature, carved so that the hooves, horns, and nostrils, even the muscles that rippled under its coat, looked real.

"Now, my best beloved," she said, "I watched the craftsman carve it. He took great pains and I told him all about you so that he might make it especially for Annie. And that's not only beautifully carved, it's very valuable wood too," she said.

"What kind?" I felt the pin, felt along the carved muscles. My hand had warmed it and under my thumb the wood felt alive, as if the animal were about to wake up and begin breathing.

"That's called stinkwood, Annie," she said. At that, the whole adult chorus chuckled, heads bobbed, eyes were wiped, hands were patted and pressed, and my humiliation was complete. "Thank you, it's very nice," I managed to say. While they clapped and clapped, I stood staring at the broken strap of my Aunt Louise's sandal, at her toes that gripped the soles as though she were leaning into a wind that was blowing her backwards, or trying to. Restlessness, like an itch, began inside me. If my grandmother had corrected herself, said: "Oh, please excuse me, Annie, I have made a dreadful mistake, that's called heavenwood," I would not have been comforted. My mother pinned the thing to the front of my dress and I sat there, feeling itchy and hot inside my clothes, looking at my badge, that sleek animal all carved of stinkwood and gathered for the leap.

But I didn't give up. When I'd recovered a little from my embarrassment, I worked my way close to her again and asked, "How did you talk to them?"

"Who, my best beloved?"

"The people over there." I imagined sign language, shadow-shows by the fire, figures scratched in the dirt with sticks, and all around, the jungle night – which was longer and scarier, somehow, than nights we knew – had gathered to listen.

"Some speak English," she said.

"Oh."

"And of course I learned a little of the Tschiluba language," she said. "It's a tonal language, not like ours."

"Say some of it."

She closed her eyes and began to speak, low liquid sounds, like music that asked questions, like a stream running fast over stones. On this tide, my hope returned. "Of course there were people who could talk for me too," she said. "They translated that language into English, and vice versa. We had us a big talking party once, and, oh, was it grand."

"Do they really wear, you know, those things?" I pointed to the rope with the tassles.

"Why yes," she said. "Some do. I can't explain this to you, heart of my heart, but it's the most natural thing in the world to them, to go around like that. They don't give a hoot about some things we hold very dear. To them our bodies are the coverings we wear, 'the beauty inside turned inside out,' they say."

Well, afterwards as we drove back to the motel, I turned over what she'd said like a small bead, round and polished. All that about people's bodies and what she'd called the hunter inside. I felt that a series of small but violent explosions had dislodged certain ideas I'd held without even knowing I believed them. I was being raised Roman Catholic because this was my father's faith and Mother, a Presbyterian, had promised to turn us over to the Church in return for being allowed to marry him. At least that's how she told it. So I knew all about the soul because every day in catechism class at Catholic school, we pinned her wings and studied her, worried over her condition and her future. I knew that this soul was either a rippling sheet of light, cold and distantly beautiful as the aurora borealis, or it was spotted with decay or even entirely dark, extinguished by sin. But whatever this soul might be, its life was not with roots or stinkwood or hunters, and darkness was always its death.

The summer I was sixteen, we went to a reunion of the Palmer family in the mountains up near Highlands, North Carolina. The house, which belonged to my great-aunt Martha, Grandmother's sister, had been added onto haphazardly and looked like a train wreck, a heap of boxcars lying every which way and covered with tarpaper but no boards or shingles, and screened from the road by a line of cedar trees that ran straight along the road's edge. Behind this house, Scaly Mountain reared up out of the earth. You could actually go out and touch the place where the mountain came out of the ground, and when the mountain threw its shadow over the house, it was damp and cold. Inside, the house was full of rooms where a person could go off by herself and think about things or read all afternoon without being disturbed.

In the valley between the mountain and the house, a small cold stream ran so fast it made a roaring sound, as though it were angry at being confined in such a narrow channel. Aunt Martha took her constitutional there. She'd built a small dam in the stream and every morning she descended into the stream, with her hair done in braids and wrapped over the top of her head, and for ten minutes she sat on stones below this dam and let the water pelt her shoulders. Now this water was so cold that you could not breathe when you were in it, and whatever parts of your body the water touched turned red and began to ache, and then went numb as cork. Nevertheless, I had decided that Aunt Martha, who was a clairvoyant, a medium, and an astrologer, famous in the family for her seances and levitations, for giving somebody the heebie-jeebies at every reunion, was more likely than my grandmother to tell me what I needed to know about clear calls, souls, destinies, and all the rest. So every morning just at dawn, I put on my bathing suit and followed her into the stream, and while the water poured over us like a clear cape, I gasped out my questions and she would tell me things about the psychic gifts of the Palmer side of the family, each one unique and fabulous, the gift of second sight and the ability to read destinies in the stars being first among them.

Or she would talk about what she called the spirit world and the reincarnated lives of other members of the family. My grandmother, for instance, had lived several lifetimes on the continent of Africa, which is why Martha had not been at all surprised when Grandmother had returned there, since the human soul, according to Martha, gravitates toward scenes of its former unfoldings as naturally as a seed seeks the earth. I told her about the time when the idea of my search had first come to me and about those moments when I'd felt that I was bound for a destiny that no one had ever lived before. I told her about the night when my grandmother had found me and read to me and I had felt myself leave the room and fly around the planet, a disembodied spirit, searching for its home. Martha nodded as she listened. "It doesn't surprise me in the least," she said. And as I talked I imagined the clear icy water running all through me and I thought: this is how I will feel when I arrive at my destiny, this is how it will be.

Nights, the grown-ups gathered near the line of cedar trees beside the road to reminisce about each other. The rest of us sat around on quilts on the grass. The stories they told were about each other, but it seemed to me that they all shared a common center. They were about the past but not the whole past, just special moments, those moments I was looking for, times that had been dilated somehow by a mysterious richness. Uncle Edward, they said that night, came to Macon, a scared, green boy from Statesboro, to take a job at the Bibb Mills. One day, on his lunch break, he passed the door to the weave room, and looking in he saw a woman sitting with her back to him, elbows flying, working like there was no tomorrow. "Never saw her face until later," someone remembered he'd said. "Never had to." The bare light bulb suspended over her head had made the cotton dust shine in her hair, and he'd known at that very moment, as though some hindrance to sight had been struck down and he saw not just her but something essential and radiant about her, that this woman would be his wife. As it turned out, he did marry her and she died shortly after bearing him two children, but no one seemed particularly sad about that as long as they could go to the quick sweet stream of that moment when he'd first seen her and drink deeply of the life there, the life that he saw in her and cleaved to all his days, past reason, past hope. And this was the stream, I promised myself, that I would drink from too. I lay on my back and listened and watched the stars and the fireflies, which were like stars drifting down to join us, until the entire meadow and valley and sky swarmed with light.

Meanwhile, Aunt Martha sat twisting the paisley scarf around her neck, rocking so hard her chair cracked each time she rocked. Finally, Uncle Edward's story was done and he was at peace, having been hauled around to funeral services in three states before coming to his final resting place among the family in the long slope of green hillside above the Ocmulgee River. Then Martha chimed in. "Now I have an interesting recollection for us about my sister, Mariah, and about her birth long ago in the south of the state of Georgia." I struggled up from the grass, pulling the damp quilt around my shoulders. My grandmother had gone to bed early. She was dizzy, she said, from the blood-pressure medicine she had to take six times a day. But it was better without her there; in her absence, her story expanded, took on important new dimensions.

Aunt Martha went on: "You know Mariah was born with her eyes shut tight as a kitten's and she didn't open them for three days? I would give anything to know what wonders she witnessed during those three days." As she talked, she rocked and stared out past us all in a fixed way. Now we are getting someplace, I thought, this is more like it. And it seemed as though I'd been waiting for a long time to be there at that moment while Martha stared at the night with her enormous eyes as though she were using her second sight to carry her past the first layer of things and right on into the marrow. I turned my head slowly, the hair prickling along the tops of my arms, and looked where she was looking and saw only the fireflies and the shape of Scaly Mountain, darker than the sky.

"Mariah's was a special birth, attended by special signs," Martha continued. "She was born with the caul over her head." She looked at the group of us with wide light eyes which at this moment I can still remember as the eyes of a creature staring in from somewhere outside a circle of light. "They say the caul is a sure sign that she had been granted the gift of second sight." From the line of rockers, someone protested: "Oh, Martha, go on now."

"You can't tell me it's not true," Aunt Martha snapped back. "I was present at her birth and though I was only a small child I remember it as though it were yesterday. The pity is that she's never developed this gift."

"But how do you know she hasn't?" I asked. Martha bent her long thin neck and smiled on me. She always encouraged us girls to use our minds and speak up when we had something to say.

"Hush now, Annie," someone answered. "Martha's just talking."

I sat up then; I sat very still. The damp quilt felt clammy against my skin so I shucked it off and stood up as if I'd remembered someplace I had to go. I ducked out through the cedars and onto the road that ran the length of the valley, pulling the cigarette I'd snitched earlier out of the waistband of my shorts. I lit up, inhaled deeply, tipped my head back and blew smoke up in a blue plume toward the stars. A gift. Martha had said there was a gift and it had to do with special powers. I held the cigarette between my teeth, put my hands on my hips, and looked up at the deep blue sky. "I'm ready," I said. I thought I could hear the silence that rested there between the stars. I wondered what my gift might be. I wanted it to be clairvoyance or something like it because only with this gift would I be able to penetrate the layer of troubles that seemed to lie over everything, like humid heat over Macon, and see into the heart of things. I wandered to the edge of the road where the rhododendron bushes grew. I stamped out my cigarette, leaned close to one of the blooms, opened my eyes very wide, and stared until I started to get a headache, waiting for that flower to reveal the secret of its life. I imagined that this would happen in slow motion, like time-lapse photography – first the petals would unfold, then the center would break open and fall away and there inside I would see it: a star-swarming stream of pure life.

I gave up on the flower and I imagined myself going back to school equipped with special powers, able to know who was a real friend and who was a secret enemy, able to know the secrets people keep in their hearts and to help them with their darkest troubles. And I would know what it was that Mother and I fought about all the time and why Grandmother never spoke to Aunt Rachel except in a cold and formal tone of voice and why Aunt Louise, Mother's sister, only called us late at night, and why my father could sometimes be found sitting back in the kitchen at three o'clock in the morning without a single light turned on. Behind me, something scratched lightly in the gravel. I turned slowly, full of a tingling like the light shaking of a thousand small silver bells, ready for my first encounter with the spirit world, and found one of Aunt Martha's old palsied hounds that had shuffled out after me, wagging its lazy tail. From back at the house, a screen door slammed, my mother's voice called "Annie, Annie, come in now, please." The spell was broken.

Still, for most of the rest of the night, I tried not to sleep, because I had discovered that sleeping on it, as you're so often advised to do, makes some of the best feelings and strongest convictions dissolve into thin air. So, up in the Hen's Nest, a narrow room under the eaves where the women and girls slept, I tried to hold onto what Aunt Martha had said about the gifts, and the way I had felt out on the road waiting for mine: as though some barrier were about to crumble and I was about to see things that no human eye could see, and no tongue could tell. As it turns out, I was right about sleep. When I woke up, it seemed, I had forgotten everything. Martha had taken her constitutional without me and gone into town, so I went looking for my grandmother instead, to ask her about these gifts she was supposed to have and why she'd never developed them, as Aunt Martha had accused her of not doing.

It was then that trouble lifted its head. I wandered through the house listening for the sound of my grandmother's voice. In the living room, a picture window looked out onto Scaly Mountain. Someone had placed an ink bottle full of violets on the windowsill, right below the teardrop-shaped crystal that Martha had hung in the window. Crystals, Martha said, are excellent conductors of the life force. I tapped it and small rainbows wobbled all over the walls and ceiling.

I found them in the kitchen. My grandmother was wiping her eyes with the back of one hand and fanning a newspaper over the cakes with the other. My mother chopped cabbage on the drainboard beside the sink, her mouth as thin and set as the blade of her knife. Aunt Louise's name, like the echo of an angry outburst, hung in the air. I perched on the stool beside the table, grabbed a knife and a head of cabbage, and began to chop. There were travel brochures fanned out on the table. They showed New England on a vivid autumn day, all red and orange, with a silver bus cutting cleanly down a road, sun exploding off the windshield beneath a sky so clear you might break chunks from it.

Grandmother was keen on taking fall foliage tours in New Hampshire and Vermont. Every year she went and sent us postcards covered with lists of the colors she'd seen, which sounded to me like no colors ever seen on this earth — heliathin, saffron, beaten gold — all brought to an absolute *pinnacle* of beauty in their last days of life. If Louise could just be there and see it, surely it would do her heart good, surely she would thrive in that good clean air. Surely the trip would bring her back to herself. I tried to match this vision of Louise with the woman I knew, the one who hadn't been able to come to the reunion because she had sprained her ankle or something. The Aunt Louise who sat restlessly silent at any gathering, worrying at her hands, the woman who walked as though she were a globe turning around a bent axis. Oh no, not that Louise. My grandmother shooed her off with the newspaper. This other Louise was revived, refreshed, she was a risen Louise who laughed like a girl, who drank all the clear sweet water she wanted to drink. "Is Aunt Louise sick?" I asked.

"Just worn down, honey," my grandmother said. "She's had such a long, trying summer, you see."

"Louise has had several trying *winters* too," my mother snapped. "In fact, if you ask me, her summers and winters are getting worse every single year."

"Well, it's a good thing no one's asked you," my grandmother said. She flipped open a brochure and frowned at an autumn hillside. The newspaper swept back and forth across the cakes.

"Let's just look at some facts here, Mother," she said. There's no stopping Mother when she's in full cry. As usual when Mother talked facts, I wanted to yell loud enough to drown her out. Her facts were always strong medicine, mixed in a dose equal to your high opinions of yourself and others. I cringed to see her number Louise's failures: the three lost jobs, the falls, the near-accidents, the calls, the *collect* phone calls to my mother in the middle of the night. Grandmother hunched over, guarding something with her body.

"You're free to make of this what you will," she said.

"Thank the Lord for independent minds. But Louise is my daughter. You're not there. I am. And she needs me."

"Will somebody please tell me what's wrong with Aunt Louise?" I said.

My mother fixed me with her long, contemplative stare with which she seems to be staring into a void full of the world's sadness. "She drinks," Mother said wearily. "She should be put in a hospital where she can get help."

"Her life is hard," my grandmother said, smacking the table hard with her palm. "She has a difficult life. Her husband and her children are unmanageable. And Louise will never go to a hospital as long as I'm alive." She spoke these words so clearly it seemed she'd bitten them out of all possible words on the subject.

Backing away, my mother shrugged and bit her lower lip; then she began to chop cabbage, letting the blade come too close to her hand. "Louise is a wreck," she said quietly. "It's just plain cruel not to see it."

"Louise is my daughter. It doesn't matter what she is, I'm with her."

I put down my knife. "Excuse me," I said, and I left the kitchen, fighting down the urge to run. I went and stood on the porch, blinking into the strong sunlight. Did Aunt Louise have gifts, I wondered. If so, what happened to them? What was it that wrecked inside you? Where did you go when you were lost, and where did you come back to when you were found?

That fall, as she had promised, my grandmother took Aunt Louise to New England for a foliage tour. And, as my mother had predicted, the trip was a disaster. The Louise my grandmother had imagined — the revitalized, healed

Louise who would find inspiration, comfort, peace, something bright in herself to match the leaves — that Louise, when taken to the mountains, vanished from the tour. She was found two days later holed up in an expensive hotel without two dimes to rub together. "The room-service tab was all for liquor, Annie," my mother said. "Louise was dead-dog drunk." Mother's cheeks were flushed, her eyes bright. When she looks that way it's easy to imagine her on a horse, leading a crusade. The story of the crisis, as it developed via the long-distance telephone line, was this: on the morning when they came within sight of the most spectacular gorge in the White Mountains, a deep gorge with sides so thickly wooded and blazing that the air seemed saturated with color, as though the world they'd come into at last were one tall flame, Louise bolted. The last person to see her reported that she was weeping. She'd checked into the resort hotel where they found her, started drinking, and — since she couldn't pay and she couldn't leave without paying — she stayed, and kept ordering out for liquor.

The ashtray on the phone stand filled up with Mother's cigarette butts as she negotiated the return of her mother and sister to Georgia. I hung around waiting for the progress reports and feeling helpless. I'd grown up believing there was always *something* you could do. She slammed down the phone: "Annie, she took Louise out and bought her a new dress and then she led her around like a little lost child, just like a little child. Can you beat that?"

I said I couldn't. It seemed some things couldn't be helped. Aunt Louise was one of them. My grandmother seemed defeated by it. She telephoned us when she got home. I ran to the back of the house and grabbed the extension phone, in time to hear her say: "Louise has so much to give, I wanted to remind her of that. I thought she might see it this time."

"Well, she didn't," my mother said.

"Why didn't it help?" I asked my grandmother. I couldn't keep the anger out of my voice. After all, *she* was the one who was supposed to know about everything.

Her voice sounded tired, as though she'd sunk to the bottom of a deep, hollow place. "There is something in Louise that nobody can get to," she said. "Don't ask me why."

I heard my mother take a breath. I thought I would kill her if she said anything small or mean-spirited. "Well, Mother, you tried," she said finally.

"And I will continue to do so," she said. "You can count on that."

I didn't exactly lose touch with my grandmother after that fall, but over the next six years it seemed we had to reach across a wider gap in order to make contact. There were the letters, always, and the Christmas visits when Louise wasn't doing too badly and my grandmother could leave Macon. But in the November following the reunion, Martha died, the mountain house was sold in April, and after that the family split off into separate orbits, each around a different sun.

I knew my grandmother was sick and getting sicker but it didn't seem exactly real to me. I only knew that by the time I graduated from college, my grandmother was seriously ill with angina. Her life had become a series of risks. "Washing dishes or bathing," she wrote to me once, "are now gambles

I must take. For my efforts, I'm rewarded with a freely drawn breath or with these chest pains."

Early in July, I was visiting at home when Aunt Louise was involved in her second hit-and-run accident of the year, and the judge gave her a choice: she could sign herself into a hospital for alcoholics, or she could go to jail. When my mother heard that my grandmother had consented to Louise's hospitalization, she said: "We are going to see Mother, *today*."

It was an edgy drive, a cord of silence tied in small knots of talk. We drove down through Georgia, through Thompson and Sparta, the dusty towns bunched around their courthouse squares. Some had limp red and green tinsel left over from Christmas, faded and unseasonable, still wrapped around the light poles. We spoke only twice during the drive. Leaving Thompson, she said: "You be sure to tell her you're getting married."

"Of course," I said. "Why wouldn't I?" Later, when we stopped for the traffic light in Sparta, I said: "Is she very sick?"

My mother gunned the engine until the fan belt screeched. "Yes," she said. The light changed from red to green, and she pressed the accelerator firmly. I felt as though we'd spoken to each other for the first time in years.

The apartment house where my grandmother lived hadn't changed. Neither had the hill where the building stood. Only the trees lining the sidewalk had changed, their tops sawed flat to make way for the power lines. We opened the heavy oak door that always stuck and walked inside. In the hallway, the smell of gas and bacon grease still lingered. The tea roses on the stained wallpaper were brown.

We let ourselves into her living room. It looked like one of those rooms in a museum, arranged to show the clutter and hurry of someone's everyday life. Her reference books and composition books with their black and white mottled covers were piled beside chairs, slips of paper sprouting from between their pages. Dust lay thick on every surface and the windows were clouded, streaked with dried rain. All the walls were hung with African paintings, carved copper crosses, the shaman's mask with its leopard-skin face now moth-eaten, mournful as the face of a derelict.

Her nightstand was covered with pill bottles, and a chart hung from a string around the bedpost with check marks beside the hours and the names of pills. She lay dozing on the bed, one arm flung over her eyes, dressed as though she were going to a party, in a lavender print dress with purple beads and earrings to match. She'd dotted her cheeks with two bright circles of rouge and brightened her mouth with lipstick. But her feet were bare, the blue veins like forked branches all over them, the toenails thick and stained tobacco-brown. I reached for my mother's hand. And as I watched my grandmother's chest rise and fall with each breath, I realized that Mother and I were matching our breathing to hers, and I thought I understood a little more about what people mean when they say "This person is alive." They mean that the circle curves, unbroken, between what is visible and what cannot be seen, and you know of its existence the same way you know currents in water by watching a boat or currents in the sky by seeing the way a hawk holds tight to the wind. I let go of Mother's hand and went to the window and yanked at the dusty blinds, forced the window open as high as it would go. The sound of a jackhammer riddled the air. Still, she lay quietly, breathing from somewhere high in her chest.

"Mother."

"Grandmother." Mother and I spoke at once. For a second or two, she stared at us wildly, as though we were robbers. She sat up, one cheek creased and flushed, and fumbled at the nightstand for her glasses. I helped her with her slippers and then she stood up beside the bed and reached for us. She'd lost weight and her dress hung on her in folds, like a slack flag. I was her best beloved, she said, my mother was the light of her life. She pressed her hand to her chest and began to take small sips of air.

"You sit down," Mother said, her forehead tight with worry. We helped her to the armchair in the living room and she sat heavily. "I'll make us some tea," Mother said, in her voice that gets cheerful and bright whenever she's afraid.

"Coffee for me," I said. "Black, please." Grandmother started to protest. She leaned up in her chair, then let herself go against the cushions. And I saw that she was radically changed. It was as if I'd been looking at her from the corner of my eye and had finally gotten up the nerve to look her full in the face. And for a moment, whatever hurries us along, slipping one minute into the next to make a continuous flow of time, stopped, and I had my moment of sight, though it was no gift I would have asked for. Her face looked vivid and full of light, as though her expression had become a clean window, and peace itself looked through. And then, without pause or change, her face began to darken into a stillness beyond peace, beyond any power to name or know. But that light didn't just disappear — I saw it leave her. And it seemed at that moment that death was very close to us, only it wasn't silent or empty or dark. It was full of the recollection of everything I had loved about her, everything that would be lost, as though grief and love are the fruit of the same tree, the one with roots so old and tangled they can never be pulled apart.

I turned away then. I think I twisted away, because she grabbed my wrist and held it. Her hand felt strong, as though she'd gathered all her strength there. "Well, sit right down," she said, "and tell me how it is."

"How is what?" I felt confused, and let myself be pulled into the chair next to hers.

"Oh the wide, wide world and those who live there."

"It's about the same," I said. I rubbed her hand, felt the knuckles under the loose skin, moved my thumb over the joints.

"Now you know as well as I do that that is never so," she said. She closed her eyes, her head dropped back. I saw her face settle along the bones into that stillness. When she opened her eyes again, she looked angry and scared. "Lulluraburg," she said. She shook her head. "That name has eluded me for days."

"The place where they sang?"

She smiled. "Imagine remembering that from when you were just a little thing."

"I think there's lots I remember," I said. "Pieces of it come floating back to me now and then, like there's a place for them, you know what I mean?"

"I do indeed," she said. "I do indeed. And aren't you looking well! Your mother tells me you're just doing so well."

"Yes," I said, "yes I am." The sound of my voice was loud with cheerfulness, just like my mother's. "I'm getting married soon."

"Married?" She turned her head so quickly I thought a sound had startled her. She looked at me fiercely. "Is he a good man, and I mean day-to-day?" She tapped out the words on the arm of the chair with one long finger.

"Why yes," I said. "Yes he is, as a matter of fact. How did you know? Now don't forget, the wedding's in August. I want to make sure you don't miss it. I'll drive down and pick you up, how would that be?"

"Married," she said. "Isn't that something!" She folded her arms and looked straight ahead. "The Bible says it's not good that we should be alone, because if one should fall alone, who will pick him up, and if one should lie alone in the cold, who will warm him?" She picked at a loose thread on the arm of the chair. *You haven't answered my question, will you come to my wedding?* I wanted to say, but just then my mother returned with a rattle of cups and saucers, calling: "Here we are now, isn't this nice?"

I let go of her hand and excused myself. I went into the bathroom and stood at the window looking across what had been a trash-filled gully, now grown over in kudzu and wild Cherokee rose. The chinaberry tree was still standing, hung with dull gold fruit, half choked in dead limbs. As I watched, a cardinal snagged in the upper branches and began its high sweet chirping. The Ocmulgee wound by, a thick and sluggish muddy gold, and I thought of the summers I'd spent there watching the river, following it in my mind's eye all the way down till it found the Atlantic. I used to stand there imagining myself in a small glass-covered boat drifting down the river, and when I talked to her about this trip I wanted to make, my grandmother was always ready to go. Sometimes while I helped her dry the dishes, we stocked my boat with provisions — matches in a waterproof case, canned food, a cat for good company, a map. She'd laughed. "You don't need a map."

"Well, what if the river forks?"

"Well, what if it does?"

Around five o'clock my grandmother refused for the last time to come back with us to South Carolina. "This is my home," she said. "I have work to do here."

"What work?" Mother snapped. She thrust her chin out the way she does and I saw how she must have looked as a child, challenging someone whose protection she needed, whose power she feared.

"I have to prepare my YWCA classes for fall," my grandmother said in that cold, imperious tone that allowed no words to follow.

My mother shoved a cigarette into her mouth and bustled around the apartment, bullying things into place, shoving books and papers around, slapping at the dust with a rag, stirring it up so it hung in the air. When she finished and we'd collected our things, she said: "Now, Mother, for goodness' sake call us. You just worry me to death." She laughed, her mouth open, and said: "Oh well, Mother, what would we do if everybody was as stubborn as you?"

"I'm glad I have a tractable nature," I said. I laughed too.

Grandmother hauled herself out of her chair and stood there breathing, counting, as though she were poor and every breath was a dollar she was forced to spend.

"Mother, don't come out with us, we can let ourselves out," my mother said. But she walked with us anyway, as far as the entrance to the building. I turned and waved as we walked down toward the car. "August," I yelled. "I'll come and pick you up. You'll like him, I promise, he's your type." She cupped her hand to her ear, nodded. At the car, I shaded my eyes and looked back, hoping to find her gone, but she was still there, standing quietly and watching the clouds, the trees along the street, in a shy sort of way as though she'd just noticed the size and silence of things. She stared at me as though she were looking for a bird in a tree. Then deliberately and clearly she said "Goodbye," and she turned and walked back into the building.

It wasn't until four summers later, when Grandmother was four years dead and my daughter Jesse was three, that I came to a place I recognized again as a destination on some road I had been traveling, though I couldn't tell you all the twists and turns that brought me there. What happened was that Mother came down with pneumonia in the middle of August. It came on her overnight while my father was away on business in Mobile, and what was so frightening was the timing of it. When she called to tell me, the sky was white, the sun glared off the sidewalks, the thermometer read ninety-seven degrees. She couldn't say just exactly what was wrong, probably nothing, or why she hadn't called one of her friends there in town, but she was having trouble breathing and she just felt, well, weak and sort of cold, not all the time, but whenever she moved around. Why, yesterday, if I could imagine such a thing, she had gotten so dizzy that she'd just had to lie down for a minute, right there on the kitchen floor. She sounded casual about it, the way you might with a stranger in the house and you calling for help and trying not to let on that you were afraid of him.

People don't get pneumonia in the middle of August, I said to myself as I drove to South Carolina. That's just crazy. It was close to dusk by the time I made it. When I opened the door, the heat hit me like a blast of desert air. The temperature in the house must have been eighty degrees. Mother had camped out under a pile of blankets on the sofa back in the den. With the curtains drawn, the room was dark as a lair, the only light came from the television set on the table in front of the sofa. Her eyes watched me from a shadowed place way back in her head. I put my hand on her forehead; it was so hot the heat seemed to radiate from it. "What took you so long?" she asked, her voice high and wheedling as an old woman's.

"I've been on my way ever since you called, Mother," I said. "I came as soon as I could." I yanked back the curtains, cranked open the window. As the light came into the room I saw how old she looked, how scared. I saw on her face the same dimness I had seen on my grandmother's face just before she died. It looked as though her cheekbones were throwing shadows under the skin. And I felt ashamed just then, for the trust I had put in the future, the way I always looked beyond what was right in front of me, believing that my destiny was somewhere else. For that blind burrowing trust that tunneled toward some promised land where we would all arrive someday, together and healthy and whole. For that misplaced faith in a someday when all would be well, all promises kept, all gifts given, all life lived.

"At least you're here now," she said. Her eyes closed and I pressed her hand to my cheek and held it there.

"Let's go," I said. "We're going to the emergency room right now." She was too weak to change out of her house-dress, but while I called her doctor to meet us at the hospital, she pulled on the fur coat my father had given her and together we went down into the August heat. There was something awful about the sheen of that healthy-looking fur wrapped around her and the way she shivered inside it as though she were shivering from a place that nothing could warm.

I called my father in Mobile. Then, for three days, while I waited for him to come home, I took prescriptions to the drugstore and doled out the medicine, cleaned the house and watered the flowerbeds. For some reason I got it in my head that what she needed was fish, fresh vegetables, and clear broth with lots of ginger in it. So I went to the market and bought bunches of greens, tiny lady peas and lima beans, okra and tomatoes and corn with the milk still sweet in the kernels. Every day I bought fresh shrimp or grouper or flounder, food from the ocean, with the ocean's mineral brine in the sweet flesh. "I'm going to swim out of here by the time you get through with me," she said.

"That's the idea," I said. I watched while the shadow retreated from her face. On the third day, her fever broke, her eyes cleared.

The night before my father was due back from Mobile we sat up late back in the den while a summer storm moved onto us. I was paging through back issues of *Southern Living* while Mother read, an afghan across her lap to guard against the chills that still shook her now and then.

The air thickened and grew stuffy, bringing the charge of the storm into the room to surround us. The rain blew in scattered gusts. Then, with a stumble of thunder, the tall hickory tree just outside the window bent halfway to the ground and the windows rinsed with rain as though a bucket of water had been thrown against the glass. I held the magazine up in front of my face and tried to focus my attention on the chart on the page that showed how to schedule your fall garden chores: when to take in the gladiola bulbs, how deep to plant next spring's jonquils.

I tried to concentrate but all I heard was the rain as it rushed around the house, around the room where we sat watching, and the wind as it bent the trees and whipped the leaves. Then a gust of wind came that was so strong it made the weather stripping hum under the door. I dropped my magazine and looked up and that's when I saw my startled face staring back from the window. At the sight of my own scared face, something gave way inside me that had been holding firm since I'd first arrived and seen how sick my mother was. Behind me, Mother read as though she did not hear the storm, as though she would read forever. But the storm was everywhere and I thought that if I listened long enough, I might hear the sound of the rain as it came into the house and ran inside the walls like a river, and the sound of the house going under that river, dissolving board by board, life by life, until all had been returned that once had been given.

I bowed my head again and turned through the pages, trying to find something that would hold my attention. And when I had skimmed through every page and looked up again, I saw myself again in the window glass and

Mother behind me, with her book closed over one finger and her head turned toward the sound of the storm. And I saw that the dullness had left her face. She was well again, and unafraid.

"Some storm," she said, as though she could match it, strength for strength, blow for blow.

"The best part of a storm is when it's over," I said. Already, the storm had wheeled away to the south. The gap lengthened between lightning and its thunder. Outside, I heard the trees dripping. It was over. But when the time came, I felt no peace. I looked to my mother, trying to find comfort in her health, in the light that had returned to her face. Instead, I saw in this light everything I had ever rejoiced in, grieved over, loved. There was nothing outside it, nothing beyond. And I saw that this life I had tried to find and know and keep exists in this world in human form, and darkened by the crossing. And on the banks of that river I bowed my head, thankful for the night and the rain and the trouble, and for the darkness in which the light is kept.

Seeing Aunt Louise again was what started me thinking about all this again. I'd driven down to Macon for the day to do research in the Mercer Library and she'd asked me to stop by for a visit. I hadn't seen her in years, not since Grandmother had died, so I wasn't prepared for the change in her. The Louise I remembered had been dazed and frumpy-looking. But the Louise who answered the door was thin and dressed in a buff suede tunic and sweater and matching shoes. She looked thin but not starved. In fact, she looked healthy and solid, alive. I remembered what my mother had said after seeing Louise up on the dais, the guest of honor at her fourth AA birthday party. "I felt like I was celebrating right along with her," she'd said. Seeing Louise again, I felt that same kind of rejoicing, so quiet it couldn't be named, running like a stream through her life. "Louise," I said, "you're looking so well." We held each other's elbows while she considered this.

"That's because I *am*," she said.

Louise's place is modern and it overlooks the river. She's done it up with a lot of glass: glass shelves, glass ornaments, each set on a chosen spot and with a little pool of space around it as though everything needed room to breathe. Louise moved within a quiet space of her own. As we talked, her hands stayed calm in her lap. But it was her face that told the story. Nothing had deserted her face, not the pain and not the death. It was all there like something you could read if only you knew the language. There was the death she'd lived and the life that came after that death, all shadowed by a determination that was almost, but not quite, peace.

We sipped our coffee and traded pictures – my daughter Jesse and my husband Thomas, her grandson, William, Jr. Finally, I said: "It's getting late, Louise. Thomas and Jesse expect me for supper." But neither of us moved.

She said: "Will you look at something before you go? I found this the other day and I can't for the life of me figure it out." She hauled out her mother's African scrapbook, the one covered in woven straw and embroidered on the front with a wine-red moon, a golden sun. We flipped through the pages – past the pressed fronds and African flowers, the snapshots of the Mountains of the Moon, the scroll signed by Neptune – and stopped at a child's crayon drawing done in yellow, black, and green, of people in a jungle gathered around a snake. My grandmother was among them, the pillow-shaped person wearing black shoes and glasses. "I know that's supposed to be Mother," Louise said, "but what's that?"

"A dead snake?"

"I know that," she said. "I'm talking about the other thing."

The snake's eyes were red *x*'s, the forked tongue lay limply on the ground. Out of its middle, an animal was rising, a cross between fox and deer, with wings and a fishy smile, surrounded by a globe of light. "Oh that," I said, sorting back through the Africa stories. "Isn't that the anaconda they found that had swallowed some kind of animal?"

Louise laughed. She put her hand to her throat. "How could I forget?" she said. "Of course that's right. The animal that was alive inside the snake." She shook her head. "Now, who do you suppose made that one up? Mother was always so serious about it too."

"Maybe she made it up."

"Maybe she did. She was good at that." Louise's smile tightened. "She surely was."

By the time I left Macon, dusk lay thick as blue dust over the fields. It was autumn then, and in the dusty green woods the sourwood leaves had already turned a lustrous red. All the way home I thought about these things, turning them over in my mind, putting one turn next to the other, watching the road they made. It seemed like one road with many turnings and the end nowhere in sight. When I got to the outskirts of Atlanta, the traffic started to pick up, and I turned my attention toward home. I imagined how Jesse would look, waiting for me at the front window, and how she'd rush out as soon as she saw the car coming down the street and dance around me while I unloaded the car, talking a mile a minute. "What'd you bring me?" I could almost hear her say. "Where'd you go, how long did it take you? What'd you bring me?"

Well, Jesse, I will say, I have those ivory elephants that march across the mantle in single file, the big ones first, the little ones following. I have the wooden bowl with the people carved at the bottom, the ones who are passing the ivory bird from hand to hand. And now I have this story to tell, to keep you through the night and give you good dreams. I will say: In Africa, Jesse, your great-grandmother was walking beside the Kasai River one day and she stepped over a log lying across the path, and do you know, that log was a snake? Yes it was. Well, that old snake lifted up its old scaly head and its eyes looked cold and dead, like the eyes of a very sad person. And this snake wanted to swallow her whole, it surely did. How did she know? She saw it in his eyes. When she saw the snake, why of course she yelled as loud as she could. And some men heard her and they ran out from the village and they killed the snake. Yes they did. They killed it, and they cut the snake open and do you know what they found? They found an antelope fawn that the snake had swallowed. It stood up trembling, Jesse, and do you know, that creature was alive? Yes. Down inside that dark old snake, it was alive as you or me.

A NOTE ABOUT THE AUTHOR

Pam Durban grew up in South Carolina. She has
worked as a journalist and teacher in New York, Ken-
tucky, and Georgia. She was the 1984 recipient of the
Rinehart Award in Fiction, and her work has appeared
in a number of publications, including *The Georgia
Review, Tri-Quarterly,* and *Crazyhorse.* The title story
of this, her first book, appeared in *The Editor's Choice*
anthology, Vol. II. She currently teaches at Ohio
University in Athens, Ohio.

ALL SET ABOUT WITH FEVER TREES

has been composed by Roy McCoy, Cambridge, Massachusetts, in Linoterm Sabon, a face designed by Jan Tschichold. The roman is based on a fount engraved by Garamond and the italic on a fount by Granjon, but Tschichold introduced many refinements to make these models suitable for contemporary typographic needs. Designed by Dede Cummings Carmichael, the book was printed by The Alpine Press, Stoughton, Massachusetts, on Warren's #66 Antique, an entirely acid-free sheet.